Bangalored

Gayatri Chandrasekharan

Leadstart
INKSTATE

ISBN 978-93-5438-876-7

First published in India 2021 by Leadstart Inkstate
A Division of One Point Six Technologies Pvt Ltd

119-123, 1st Floor, Building J2, B - Wing,
Wadala Truck Terminal, Wadala East,
Mumbai 400022, Maharashtra, INDIA
Phone: +91 96999 33000
Email: info@leadstartcorp.com
www.leadstartcorp.com

Disclaimer: The views expressed in this book are those of the Author and do not pertain to be held by the Publisher.

Editor: Kavya Shree
Cover: R. Maharaja
Layouts: Kshitij Dhawale

For Appa

And to Bengaluru

About the Author

After a 20-year career in the corporate world, Gayatri Chandrasekharan has begun to indulge her love of writing. She loves nothing better than to curl up with a cup of tea, surrounded by her three dogs and read her favourite books.

She is a Chemical Engineer from RV College of Engineering, Bangalore, and an alumnus of the Indian Institute of Management, Lucknow.

Present Day

'Tis better to have loved and lost than never to have loved at all.

Lord Alfred Tennyson

The weather really seemed to match her mood. Sombre. Dark. Furious. Lashing rains and viciously biting monstrous winds whooshed past reminding her of her own acid tongue. Occasional streaks of lightning illuminated broken tree trunks. She really ought to turn back or find shelter but it was as if some contrary being within her urged her to carry on and court disaster. Lucifer was giving her his usual inclined-head, non-plussed look of *these humans are crazy*. Lucifer she could count on; he might not always get her, but he would never leave her side even if it meant being thrown from side to side as she swerved to avoid the potholes on the streets of Bangalore. She drove like a person possessed, her car splashing water onto the sidewalk but no one was there to berate her. Most people apparently had better sense than to walk on the streets in this weather. But most people hadn't had their heart broken. Most people hadn't been devastated by the cards life had dealt them. She was suddenly reminded of her father. He would make a distinctive action of someone dealing cards and say that one just had to pick up the cards and play them, no matter how good or bad they were. *Well…* His 'take it on the chin' approach was all very well but it felt terrible to pick up a bad set of cards, as any gambler would swear. She believed she had earned the right to whine. It was certainly better to have never loved at all than to have loved and lost. She hoped Lord Alfred *bloody* Tennyson was turning in his grave.

Somehow the car moved, as if exercising its own muscle memory, inexorably towards Attara Kacheri. It seemed ironic that this is where she should stop—the High Court of Karnataka—when life had not deemed it fit to see any justice done to her. The wry smile came once again. She could really be as dramatic as the next person, couldn't she?

She parked her car and walked, shivering and dripping wet, to the pavement and sat down. Never before had she sat down on a pavement, but if an occasion demanded a breaking from the ordinary, it was this. Lucifer looked at her disdainfully and kept standing. But he could be as uppity as he wanted, she was not getting up. She had thought things were in control, that she had put the pain in her heart behind her, that she was past caring. Until today. And then, unmindful of the inclement weather, she got into her car and had been drawn here.

She noticed someone in the distance emerge from the sheet of rain. Lucifer let out a low growl, but she was not scared. As long as Lucifer was with her, no one could harm her. As the person started walking with slow steps towards her, Lucifer's growl turned into a whine of recognition and a sharp bark of happiness. And then, his tail started wagging vigourously.

"You!"

CHAPTER 1

Nine Months and a Few Days Ago

Hell has no fury, it is well-known, like a woman who wants her tea and can't get it.

P G Wodehouse

Radha Iyer sipped her morning coffee as MS Subbalakshmi's *Suprabhatham* played in the background. She didn't particularly care for coffee. Her idea of heaven was tea and she strongly believed that coffee smelt far better than it tasted. But she was not going to argue with her Tamil brahmin family on an enduring morning routine—*Suprabatham* played every morning and as one listened to MS' clear-as-a-bell voice wake Lord Vishnu, one sipped strong coffee. That was all there was to it. Radha later made her special brew of tea, but first thing in the morning had never been a good time to argue the relative merits of hot beverages with her belligerent family. One needed to pick the battles one wanted to fight, and when to fight them.

She could afford her meandering thoughts on coffee, family and war strategy today. She had taken off from work and was damned if she was going to check her email or respond to phone calls. A day of nothingness stretched beautifully in front of her as she tucked her long legs beneath her and picked up the crossword. Lucifer nudged himself closer to her and stretched on his back in a clear order to Radha to stroke his belly. For the millionth time she marvelled at the expression *it's a dog's life*. If she could, she would exchange her life with Lucifer's in a second. All he did was eat and sleep. At other times, people were either fussing over him or cleaning up after him and the slightest annoyed bark from him had everyone in the house in a tizzy, rushing to offer him every comfort and treat to make sure his tantrum abated. Lucifer watched her from the corner of his eyes accusingly as if to say, "Don't begrudge me my existence. I can't help it if the lot of you are enamoured of me. Charm's my thing!"

After wrapping up the crossword with an eight-letter word for an illicit lover and finishing an invigorating yoga and meditation session, Radha sat down to her breakfast of steaming hot idlis and spicy coconut chutney. She never did believe in a cereal and fruit breakfast. What was the point of living in South India if one didn't make the impossible choices between dosa, idli and upma on a daily basis? Her phone rang. It was Alex, her colleague from work. It was no use trying to ignore the insistent ringing. She knew she would pick it up sooner or later as she was cursed with the vilest of foibles— conscientiousness. And so, with a deep sigh and donning her most unfriendly tone, she picked up and said hello.

"Hey, Radha! Am I bothering you?"

Radha rolled her eyes. She loved Alex. She counted him as being amongst her closest friends rather than a colleague. But he had the annoying habit of stating what was patently obvious.

"Of course, you are, you nitwit! Didn't I tell you I was off work today? Somebody better have died for you to be bothering me."

"Always with the unthinking flippancy, huh, Radha? Someone did *actually* die. My maternal grandmother."

Radha bit her tongue but this was Alex and she hadn't known him for three years for her to apologize for being herself. "How's aunty? How can I help?"

"You know that big sales deal I'm working on? The client is visiting from the UK this week and I'm leaving with my mom for Kerala in a few hours. I need you to stand in for me, Radha. Pretty please and all that jazz."

She groaned at the thought of the extra work but when one's friend asked for help, one gave it unhesitatingly. "Okay. Drop by my place and brief me on what's happened so far and what outcome you want achieved during your get-rich-deal client visit. On the condition that half the bonus you make on this deal is mine."

"Done! Love you. See you in a bit. And whip up something for me to eat when I'm there, won't you?"

Radha ruefully put away the remnants of the breakfast and called her friend of many years. "Hey, Lakshmi! I'm going to have to ditch our lunch plans today. Duty beckons. Need to stand in for Alex at work over the next few days and I need to be briefed by him."

"As long as you don't end up consorting with his briefs."

"Don't be ridiculous! You have an absolutely juvenile sense of humour and a dirty, one-track thought process that goes for a mind."

"But you love me."

Radha could almost see the pout that would have followed this statement as she replied, "Only because you latched on to me like a leech since we were six. Honestly, what choice did I have in the matter?"

"Touché! What happened to Alex the Hunk?"

Radha rolled her eyes for the second time in quarter of an hour. Lakshmi was impossible. Didn't she already have her hands full with the numerous boyfriends she juggled and the numerous others who were always waiting on the sidelines to pour out their love for her in prose or poetry or painting or whatever little talent they possessed? Lakshmi seemed to turn men into witless fools around her. Had it been another woman, Radha would have wanted to claw her eyes out in pure envy, but this was her dearest, most perfect friend. One who would lay down her life for Radha. *And probably drive half a dozen men to suicide if she did*, Radha thought with a laugh.

"Pray tell what amuses you," said Lakshmi, bringing Radha back from her reverie.

"You do. Any*hoo*, lunch is cancelled. Catch you sometime later in the week."

Radha was sorry to have missed her lunch date with Lakshmi. Theirs was a friendship that had stood the test of time. From being besties in kindergarten, when they had cried to go to each other's houses after school, to middle school where they had shared lunches and heartbreaks, to senior school where they had stood as rocks for each other through the stressful world of exams, choosing streams, applying to colleges, getting rejected, to looking for their first jobs, it had all been together. There was a time when Radha was away at hostel when her mom had fallen seriously ill and it had been Lakshmi who sat with Radha's mom, handing her water and medicines, serving her food, keeping her company. Even though there had been brief periods of time when they had been in different cities and not in regular touch with each other, their relationship had never been strained. They could pick up the phone after a year of not talking to each other and pick up the conversation like neither had been away.

Now, of course, they were in the same city. They had reached the stage when people outgrew their childhood friendships, but theirs had only gotten stronger. Radha always looked forward to catching up with her. Lakshmi had a devil-may-care attitude that she was in awe of. Nothing disturbed her calm and she reminded Radha of a cat—always landing on her feet. Radha decided to stop her wandering thoughts and pulled out her laptop. If she was anyway going to work, thanks to Alex, she might as well clear her emails. There was no rest for the wicked.

*

Radha looked up from the notepad she had been scribbling on as Alex rattled off the details of his client visit. The deal was obviously indecently huge and would earn him an enviable reputation in the sales team should it come through. Not to mention the giant bonus he would make! Radha had her work detailed for the next week: preparation with her team the next day, then one day of presentations to the visiting client at the Bengaluru office followed by more presentations at their Delhi office, and then a trip to Agra on the following day to charm the socks off the visiting James Rutherford, the man to impress if this deal was to be won.

"Is everything clear?" asked Alex as he nervously wrung his hands.

"Crystal. Leave it to Psmith," said Radha who could never resist quoting Wodehouse or Jane Austen or Shakespeare should the opportunity present itself.

Shortly after Alex left, Radha's mom bustled in from her outdoor chores. She flung herself on the sofa with, "I am *enervated.*"

"Can't you just say 'exhausted' like the rest of us?"

"Using plebeian language is something I always eschew," countered Revati.

Was it so difficult to say 'using common language is something I always avoid'? thought Radha as she rolled her eyes for the third time in the day. Really, it was a miracle she hadn't contracted some deadly muscular disease of the eyes with all the eye-rolling she did. Did *everyone* have such annoying relatives and friends?

Revati Iyer had a few striking idiosyncrasies. She would never use a simple English word if she could find a fancy four-syllable word in its stead, she went about the world assuming everyone owed it to her to fulfil her slightest wish, and all her energy was spent in wishing Radha marry *well*, preferably into royalty. The last had been a special bone of contention over the last couple of years since she thought Radha was over the hill and needed to take some drastic measures to find a well-heeled and aristocratic husband before she missed the marriage-bus.

Radha loved her mother, she truly did, but Revati was an acquired taste that had to be re-acquired ever so often.

Radha and her father had always ganged up on Revati and lovingly teased her. Not that it made the slightest bit of difference to Revati; she was an unstoppable force of nature, bludgeoning her way through life, unmindful of the shambles she left in her wake. Her father used to call her 'Generalissimo Supremo' after General Franco and, indeed, she was no less fearsome than him. Her sharp tongue could wither the doughtiest person. She had been a teacher in her younger days and when one particularly boisterous class of boys had tried to frighten her off by lighting a string of firecrackers in the class, she had picked it up disdainfully and thrown it out. A brave act that, forever after, won her the respect of the boys. Never again did they misbehave and Revati's class had the highest attendance from then on. In an otherwise lawless school, this was no mean feat indeed.

"I thought you were going out for lunch, Radha?"

"I was but Alex's grandmother died and he wants me to stand in for him this week. He was here to give me instructions."

"Oh! The poor dear. Give him my love." Alex was one of the few people Revati liked wholeheartedly. And that was more credit to Alex than anything else. "We can have lunch now, in that case."

"Has Usha put in curry leaves in dal makhani again?" groaned Radha, lifting the lid of the lentil dish. "You know she makes awesome South Indian food. I don't know why she can't stick to that instead of taking South Indian seasoning to the north of the Vindhyas."

Revati admonished Radha. "What have I told you about not complaining about the food when you are eating? It's both ungrateful and ungracious. Besides, I don't need to repeat my motto to you, do I?"

"Yeah, yeah, I know," sulked Radha. *"If I like the food, I'm welcome to relish it. And if I don't, I should lump it. In silence."*

"Good! Now let's eat at once. All this work has left me tired but I do want to support the cottage industry artisans and ensure they get a fair livelihood."

"And by *supporting the artisans* I assume you mean you went shopping at the handicraft exhibition that is now on in Bangalore."

"Shh!" said Revati with a conspiratorial wink. "It's our little secret."

"And what are *your* plans for today?" asked Revati as they were finishing lunch. And then, without waiting for her answer: "I just met Asha aunty and she told me about the fantastic catering at the wedding she attended last week. They had them transport chefs and vessels and the whole shebang from Chennai, apparently. I've decided to do the same for your wedding and have made a note of their number."

"Now all I need to do is find myself a groom," Radha muttered to herself as she bid a tactical retreat to her room. Some things, Radha believed, were best left unsaid. It wasn't cowardice but self-preservation.

Chapter 2

From women's eyes this doctrine I derive:
They sparkle still the right Promethean fire;
They are the books, the arts, the academes,
That show, contain, and nourish all the world.

Shakespeare (Love's Labour's Lost)

Two days later, Radha—dressed in her most flattering saree—rushed around the house picking up her laptop, her notes, her chapstick while wolfing down spoonfuls of breakfast she picked up at intermittent stops to the dining table. Lucifer looked at her accusingly since she hadn't thrown him a single scrap but Radha decided she was going to ignore the tyrant's theatrics today. Throw him a scrap and his drool would likely fly onto her pretty saree. She simply did not have the time for his tantrums today. He would not worm his way into her guilty conscience.

"Madan, I'm late!" she shouted as she got in the back of her car. Madan shrugged in his usual, insouciant way and got into the driver's seat without even a token show of urgency at Radha's distraught shout. "You are always late, madam," was his only explanation to the frustrated look Radha threw him in the rear-view mirror. She wondered if impertinence was on the job description explained to Madan when he started working for her. Was it too much to ask for a bit of deference towards the one who paid your salary? But they both knew she was lost without Madan. Between driving her and running all her errands, he had become an integral part of Radha's life and she had come to depend on him for life to be smooth sailing.

Ignoring Madan, Radha mentally went over her preparedness for the meeting. The office staff had been instructed on the logistics, the presenters had been clearly instructed on what to emphasize and what to steer clear of, the presentations were printed out and everything was in order. Radha prided herself on her capabilities as a salesperson. She was never a wholly modest person, but in her work, she took special pride. Managing clients and their visits was all about respecting the infernal devil that resided in the details, along with a charm offensive—things Radha was extremely good at. Satisfied that everything was as it should be, she decided to spend the rest of the drive to work catching up on texts from friends and opened her WhatsApp. The drive was not particularly long, but anyone who drove in Bangalore knew how far one was from one's destination was never a matter of distance but the vagaries of traffic. Ever so rarely, one zipped to the destination but usually a person's driving time was greatly dependent on the rains or a truck breakdown or how many decided to hit the road at that time.

Her school group was as active as usual. 230 messages since she checked last night. *The lot of us are jobless*, Radha chuckled to herself as she nevertheless opened the messages. It was the usual. Some lewd forwards by adults who still thought they were teenagers—*really the things that could keep boys amused!*, some bawdy comments on the afore-mentioned lewd forwards, the odd castigation from one of the group's more prudent—*prudish?*—participants and a video re-forwarded for the umpteenth time after having made its first appearance over two years ago. There was also the harmless flirtation between two old classmates which afforded a lot of amusement to the others on the group. But Radha always felt the easy back and forth between them cloaked an undercurrent of regret that their teenage attraction never blossomed to reach its potential. And that bitter sweetness added an edge to their flirtation.

Contributing to the large number of messages were the ever-present arguments on the topic of the day. Radha, as usual, jumped in with enthusiasm. She loved a good argument and sometimes took a contrary view to everyone else just to get into an argument. In fact, her family called her *Alladi* after Alladi Krishnaswamy Iyer, the famed lawyer who helped draft the Indian constitution and whose contribution and capability was acknowledged by BR Ambedkar himself. Madly encouraging her argumentative nature was her family itself. According to the Iyer family, a late morning well spent was a strident argument on some topic or the other. Passions would overrun and a casual observer would never be able to guess that the topic being discussed was wholly unconcerned with the family. The fantastic thing about it all was that at the end of the argument, which would see opposing sides not holding back any punches, everyone would attack their *thair shaadam* (a mixture of mildly seasoned yoghurt and rice, and a manna from heaven as per any self-respecting Tamil brahmin) in companionable vigour. No one would guess that just a few minutes ago, the family had been ready to tear each other's throats out. And so, for Radha, an argument was just that—an animated discussion with no quarter given but which never caused any rancour between the participants when it was done.

She finished what she thought was an argument that would have made Nani Palkhivala look on her proudly and looked up only to see they were still a way off from her workplace. She scolded Madan for not getting her to work any faster to which he commented sarcastically, in insolent Hindi, that he could consider flying over the traffic. Radha seriously considered docking a day's salary for his impudence but instead looked desperately at the time to destination as per Google Maps. However much one played a game trying to beat the estimated time shown on it, she knew it was rarely off by more than a few minutes. She was going to be really late and would probably just reach a few minutes before the scheduled start.

As she flew into the office looking back to acknowledge a colleague, she felt herself run right into a human wall and her bag and its contents went flying…

*

James Rutherford tried to steady the person who had just run into him but himself staggered as her soft perfume made his gut wrench. *Lord, he was being ridiculous!* He looked up at the girl's face to apologize. It was a mistake. His breath sucked out of him. It wasn't that the girl was uncommonly pretty, but as he looked into the eyes that seemed too large for her face, he was momentarily poleaxed. It was somehow difficult for James to string together a sentence as he took in the girl more slowly. She was more than a head shorter than him, but of course, he was uncommonly tall. Her dark hair fell becomingly around her shoulders framing her delicate face. And her frame was enveloped in the most gorgeous of sarees. What was it about the Indian saree that transformed its wearer into a sensual being when not an inch of flesh showed, wondered James.

Realizing that he was staring, he started to apologize but the girl said, "Think nothing of it! I've always been a bit of a clumsy clod, I'm afraid, and it's really my fault for hurtling through the office."

Still embarrassed at being caught staring, he blurted, "You speak excellent English!"

Oh dear, had that not come out a bit patronizing? As though he was surprised she could speak good English? *Well done, James! Way to antagonize a person after all the cultural classes you took back in England.*

"Is there any reason I shouldn't?" came the pert reply. "Especially since we were ruled by the English for so long?"

James groaned. Of course, he had offended her. "Certainly not! I apologize. I'm James Rutherford, by the way."

"I'm Radha Iyer. I believe we are meeting in the next five minutes. Alex must have told you he couldn't be here due to a personal exigency and I am standing in for him."

"Of course, see you in a bit." James groaned as he saw the girl walk away in a huff. He had been an idiot. He was visiting the office of this Indian IT partner to finalize an engagement. The last thing he should be doing was offending someone here. It was not like he was in unfamiliar territory. This was his fourth trip to Bangalore and already the hustle and bustle had become familiar to him. The blaring horns, the roads that felt like roller coasters with all the unfilled potholes, eateries dotting the roadside and...the weather. The amazing, unbelievable weather! How did it stay so perfect nine days out of ten? The people of Bangalore were truly blessed.

Discounting the mounds of garbage one saw on the road, of course, James thought distastefully. They always seemed nice, did Bangaloreans. What little he had seen of them. Kind and helpful and soft-spoken. He should know better than to go around offending them. He would have to make amends with the chit who had walked off in such a temper. Even though she had been too prickly by half.

*

As Radha walked off, she was seething. Of all the condescending things she had heard, this had to rank pretty high. But she was going to have to control her tongue. That 'ruled by the English' comment could not have endeared her to that pompous twit. This was the client they were supposed to razzle-dazzle and she wasn't going to let Alex down just because her pride was pricked. But really, did all gorgeous men have to be such jerks? James had been uncommonly tall, even for a foreigner, and his broad chest was clothed in the most tasteful of shirts. He had copper-coloured hair. The hair was probably brown*ish*-red but it had glinted red when she had looked up at his face. The well-cut trousers had hinted at muscular thighs. And his eyes! Piercing blue. They would have put Daniel Craig's eyes to shame. And Pierce Brosnan's. He looked like he belonged in a Bond movie. He also seemed to have the reserved, brooding manner of a Bond hero. The type who spoke very little. The type whose quick temper manifested as a sullen silence.

Radha chuckled and then admonished, herself. Had she just ogled a client and then wool-gathered about his movie star looks and gone on to do a character assessment after seeing someone for all of two minutes? She needed to find herself a boyfriend!

The presentation actually started off on time, Radha was relieved to note. There were none of the usual hitches she had become familiar with over the last couple of years. Like how the projector would always know the exact time to refuse to switch on or how the audio conference bridge would have a mind of its own so nobody could hear when the client was all ready and waiting or how there was always at least one person on the video conference whose computer had a problem and who could not see a shared desktop. Sometimes the irony of being in the IT services industry and still facing these challenges was killing. However, today was the exception. Everything worked, everyone could see and hear everyone else. In fact, the next couple of hours went off without a hitch. Radha thought to gauge the client's reaction but James Rutherford seemed to epitomize the British stiff upper lip. No reaction was forthcoming and though he continued to listen and ask questions, Radha couldn't help but feel he had an aloof air. As if he was tolerating the world. Worse—as if the world should be grateful for his supercilious tolerance.

During the coffee break, Radha and James picked up their coffee and walked to the balcony. James offered her a cigarette and felt his heart lurch again at the tinkling sound of Radha's dangling earrings as she gently shook her head. "The weather is lovely as always." *That's right, James,* he told himself, *stick to the weather, the traffic, the potholes, the delays.* All safe and tried and tested Bangalore topics. Anything but this inexplicable madness that had taken possession of him.

Radha checked with James if the sessions had been to his expectations and was a little annoyed with the nonchalant shrug that accompanied his affirmation. Despite the cool, non-committal response, she was a little surprised at the sensation of warm brandy that came over her when she heard his voice. Of course, she was being ridiculous. This was an indifferent, arrogant man. Alex owed her big time for this. Suffering this insufferably superior man had not been part of the bargain.

Lunch saw Radha seated opposite James in the office cafeteria. A fancy lunch had been ordered in. In almost all her client meetings, Radha abhorred this part the most. She did not understand why the "meal with the client" was such a big deal. It was not like a special appreciation for the curry du jour or the topic of the meal would ensure the client would give them the order. Were it so easy! But such a fuss was always made by Indian vendors about this. About the supposed informal chat, the bonding with the client, the meal specifics. One would have thought the precursor for winning orders was to wine and dine the client fantastically well. What was usually irksome because of the small talk that had to be made, was made even more intolerable by the discomfort Radha felt around James. She had started off wrong by taking obvious offence to his comment about her English and somehow, she felt the atmosphere strained between them. She could not lose Alex this deal and so she squared her shoulders and gave James one of her most dazzling smiles.

"I hope you aren't allergic to anything?" And then added sheepishly, "Though, of course, it's a little late to be checking on that."

She saw James stare at her with a dazed expression and wondered if she had said something wrong but he seemed to return to the conversation and said, "I'm only allergic to bad food," with a boyish smile that made Radha realize once again how handsome he was. Luckily, the awkwardness eased off and soon the conversation veered off to cricket. Radha confessed she had a special soft spot for his country's cricket team which seemed to elicit a disbelieving rising of his eyebrows. "No really," Radha insisted with a wink. "It helps that they are all so irresistibly handsome."

James chuckled. He was glad things had gotten back on an even keel. He had been feeling weird all morning since this girl had had a strange effect on him. He felt like an adolescent with a crush and had started clamming up because of the strange sensation. And, Lord, just now when she had smiled at him, he had been rendered speechless. But she was easy to talk to and very charming and amusing, and he felt himself genuinely enjoying their conversation. "So, you are pitting good looks against the talent and grit of Virat Kohli?"

"Oh no! The English team's talent is second to none. They are just very easy on the eyes as well. It's an added bonus," countered Radha with her serious expression being ruined by the twinkle in her eye. "It also annoys people around me if I support any team other than India, so I do it just to irritate them. I love being contrary."

The easy conversation continued through the meal and the discomfort that had marked the beginning of their acquaintance seemed to melt away. The schedule after lunch was pretty packed and there was hardly any time between the sessions as almost all of them overran, which Radha hoped was a good thing because James had been quite involved in the discussions. This was going to turn out well for Alex, she was sure.

When they were at the end of the day, Radha walked James to the foyer and updated him on the plans for the next day. They were going to the Delhi office and she told James she would see him at the airport well in time before the flight.

"Ciao."

"Ciao."

Chapter 3

*If adventures will not befall a young lady in her own village,
she must seek them abroad.*

Jane Austen (Northanger Abbey)

Radha entered the crowded Kempegowda International Airport the next day. Luckily, her flight to Delhi was at 8 am so the 6 am madness at the airport was behind them. But she was late. The cab driver had switched off his phone and by the time she reached the customer service and had another driver assigned, she had left 25 minutes later than planned. Considering Radha never worked with a buffer while planning airport drives times for work trips, she was very, *very* late. Her argument to herself being that since she travelled quite often, working with a buffer on each trip meant she was significantly denting her time in the world by waiting at airports if she was early. And now she was late. Served her right for being such a smart Alec. She called James and told him she was boarding late and could not meet him at the airport but would see him at the Delhi airport since he was flying business and she was flying "cattle class" as an MP had recently called the economy class. She rushed to get help from her airline's staff to get to the top of the line studiously ignoring all the glares she was getting from the other passengers who had faithfully arrived early. If ill will had any lasting effects, this day was going to go horribly. Karma was a bitch, or so she had been told. She hustled through security earning more dirty glares and rushed to the gates as she heard the PA system blare her name out.

The last bus to the flight had left, she was told at the gate when she got there panting and out of breath and the staff at the gate put her on a rickety maintenance truck that was going towards the plane. She was the last one to board the flight and as she entered the plane, the airhostess told her that the pilot wanted to speak with her. Radha nodded with dread as she moved towards the cockpit. She had no idea that pilots could pull up passengers for being late. She felt like a schoolkid walking towards the principal's office wondering how badly she would be admonished, when she saw the smiling pilot. It was Alex's friend whom she had met a couple of times. Relief coursed through her as he shook her hand warmly saying, "I heard the name of the late passenger and checked if it was you." She sheepishly stood aside as he gave swift instructions to the cabin staff to get her seated in the business class and turned back to his controls.

Radha followed the airhostess to her seat and her ignominy was complete when she saw the person in the seat next to her was James. Of course, it would be in front of him that she would look like an idiot who almost missed flights.

"Well, hello you!" she said bravely.

"So, you are the one who was holding the plane up."

"Well, it's not like they've finished everything else and were only waiting for me," Radha countered defensively.

"They are still doing the, uh, stuff…they do before take-off," she said with a wave of the hand accompanying *stuff* as she did not have a clue what it was the staff did before a plane took off.

"I thought you mentioned you were in the economy section?"

"I was. The pilot is an acquaintance. Heard my name as the last passenger to be boarded, bumped me up, and here I am."

"You *do* realize that most people who are late for flights miss their flights? They don't get rewarded with an upgrade," James said, shaking his head and smiling wryly.

Radha shrugged, because really, what else could she say? She was sure a devastating retort would come to her later when the moment had passed. Her wittiest comebacks always had a way of striking her when the moment to cut someone to shreds was long gone.

Radha wondered if it would be rude to start off on all the newspapers she had picked up as she rushed to her gate. This was the only part of travel she loved—a chance to catch up on every newspaper in the airport stands. She was itching to start off on them but this was her client. Perhaps she should attempt some polite conversation.

"So, did you have to get up very much earlier than usual to catch the flight?" As attempts at conversation went, this must rank among the lamest.

"Not really. I always am an early riser." This said by James with a superior air and Radha was reminded of most of her family. They made a big virtue of being early risers though she was yet to figure out what they achieved after getting up at unearthly hours of the morning. She was an early riser too, but she liked to think she didn't think herself above someone who chose to sleep in. Her family, unreasonably, did.

"And what do you do that early?" she asked James.

"Well, I run most days."

"Oh! You are those runner types."

James shot her a quick look. "What do you mean by 'those runner types'? And why did you say *runner* as though it were a bad word?"

Radha mentally cursed herself. Must she be so easy to read? In truth, runners annoyed her. Not that she grudged them their healthy habits but most seemed to think running put them on some pedestal. Like they were better than others. They were quite like early risers, were runners, in her opinion. But to James she said, "Nothing like that. I just don't particularly care for running myself. Makes one all hot and sweaty and out of breath and frankly there are far more pleasing ways to get hot, sweaty and out of breath."

Radha bit her tongue as she saw James start and stare at her. Did she just say that to a client? Had she completely lost her marbles?

"I like swimming," she blurted out in a desperate attempt to move the conversation away from her stupid remarks.

"I like swimming too. Looks like we finally agree on something," said James raising one eyebrow and smiling mischievously.

"I hardly think we were disagreeing."

A shrug from James. Between shrugs and nonsensical topics of conversation, her interactions with James 'high-and-mighty' Rutherford had been the furthest from what one expects client interactions to be.

"I'm just going to catch up on the news," said Radha, picking up a paper.

"And I'm just going to take a nap," countered James unnecessarily.

"Whatever," mumbled Radha sotto voce and swore not to nod off herself. She was a most inelegant sleeper with her mouth a little open and the occasional whistling of breath when she slept. She was damned if she would let a handsome man see her that way. *No*, she corrected herself, *she was damned if she would let a client see her that way.*

To her dismay, she realized a while later as the seat belt announcements woke her, she had indeed dozed off. *Damn you, Radha!*

James Rutherford turned towards her and said, "You missed the meal. But you were fast asleep and I didn't have the heart to wake you."

Was Radha imagining it or did he say that with a playful smile on his lips? Of course, he had seen her sleep with her mouth open. Well, this was mortifying! Small mercy that she had not drooled over his shirt or something.

Squaring her shoulders, she replied, "Never mind, the food is never anything to write home about."

Smiling, James countered with a wink, "As I have rarely ever written home, I cannot agree or disagree with you."

As they were disembarking, Radha couldn't help telling James, "Usually I am on the other side of the iron curtain." When he gave her a nonplussed look, she explained, "You know…behind the business class curtain which the airhostess superciliously draws looking her nose down at the ones in the economy class, making us seated there feel like we haven't quite arrived." James smiled at this and chivalrously said, "Well, if someone deserves to be on the right side of the iron curtain, it is you." Radha looked away embarrassed.

Now why did he have to say something so sweet and turn her insides to jelly?

The company driver was waiting outside, placard in hand, and they were soon bundled inside and driving through the crowded roads of Delhi.

The car eventually weaved through the heart of Lutyens' Delhi with its wonderfully green roads and classic embassies. This part of the city had undeniable beauty. The wide avenues and the numerous government offices and embassies lent a gravitas to the political hub of the country. Radha pointed out the political residents of the bungalows as they drove past. "That's our external affairs minister's home, and that's the home minister…" She never tired of this no matter how often she came to Delhi. James watched her with amusement. She looked like a little girl in a candy store: bright eyes, excited manner, barely concealed awe of her surroundings. Somehow his other acquaintances seemed jaded in comparison.

As they drove through India Gate and Rajpath, Radha pointed out the touching war memorial to servicemen in the British Indian Army. "You might find a kindred connection since it is from our colonial past," she couldn't help saying with a cheeky smile.

"So do Indians resent the British still?" asked James candidly.

"Not really. As a culture, we are people who can move on pretty quickly. We are forgiving and accepting. Though the accepting part sometimes is our downfall as we accept almost anything like corrupt politicians and bad civic amenities," Radha added with a chuckle. "And some of us do suffer from a serious colonial hangover; we love everything foreign and have a disdain for everything Indian. I'm afraid I have to lay the blame for that squarely at your country's door. They instilled in us a sense of insecurity in our own culture, languages, learning and way of life."

"And yet you support the English cricket team?"

"We all have our failings," Radha said with a shrug ignoring James' baiting tone and raised eyebrows. "So, this is where they are remembered, people who died fighting British causes." And then added, "For England, James." At his loud guffaw, Radha felt like Pollyanna—all light-hearted and breezy. Was it because she had just said things to a British client which could have offended quite a few of his fellow countrymen but he seemed not to mind? Or was it just the unthinking happiness of an adolescent crushing on the most handsome man she had ever spent so much time with. She did really feel no older than a teenager at this moment.

"So, you are a fan of 007?"

"Is there anyone who isn't?" came Radha's pert reply. "Though I do believe they have every intention of spoiling the franchise by handing over the license to kill to a woman."

James turned to her and lifted one eyebrow. "Don't tell me you subscribe to that machismo aura of Bond. Any time of the day I would have taken you for a feminist."

"Oh, I *am* quite the feminist! I just don't find the need to bat for feminism this way. Fleming wrote him as a white male. Making him a woman as a pretext for feminism is just childish. We do have a Black Widow for every Bond, right? I think equating men and women on every minute detail is not an ideal way to approach the cause of feminism. Respect for women and an unshakeable belief that they can do anything a man does if they put themselves to it, should suffice. There must be equality at a macro level, not in every little parameter."

James put both his hands up. "I'm certainly not arguing on this."

"That's a pity. There's nothing I love more than a good argument," smiled Radha wryly.

"Then I shall deny you that small pleasure," said James with a dashing smile.

They were delayed a little in reaching Radha's Delhi office because of a minor accident in front of their car. The ensuing scuffle between the motorists had held up traffic. Nobody was hurt and even the vehicles didn't seem too damaged but the motorists were in a temper and it came down to a bit of fisticuffs between the two. They were then dragged back from each other by well-meaning bystanders and the crowd eventually dispersed. James seemed a bit surprised and Radha explained to him that people in Delhi were usually a little aggressive and this was not uncommon. Radha always thought that this aggression might be a result of centuries of fighting back marauding invaders. But, of course, she was no social scientist and could not corroborate her theory.

They were soon welcomed at the office reception with a garland for James. Radha groaned to herself. She despised this show Indian companies put on for their foreign clients. What was the big deal with the lighting of lamps and garlanding of people and the smearing of reddened turmeric on their foreheads? Whom were they trying to impress with their Indian*ness*? She had not asked for any of this but she didn't want to argue with the earnest facilities manager who stood by beaming proudly at the proceedings. Never someone to be unkind, Radha gave him an encouraging thumbs up as she and James walked past him. The meetings went on for the rest of the day and by the end of which she was exhausted. The waking early to catch the flight followed by intensive discussions at their Delhi office had taken a toll on her. Worse, between meetings, she had to pay obeisance to all the folks in the Delhi office. She had no idea why *networking* was such an important part of corporate culture. It was not that she didn't like her colleagues, she did, but she preferred to treat them as just that. She did not subscribe to the view that one had to fraternize with them or be thick as thieves with them just to make sure one stayed relevant in the organization. According to her, it should suffice if one did their work and made a reasonable attempt to get along with her co-workers. This chumminess was all a bit too much for Radha as she was essentially an introverted person who highly valued solitary bliss.

Nevertheless, what couldn't be cured had to be endured and Radha made a token show of catching up with everyone. And, consequently, she was physically and mentally exhausted by the end of the day. There was the dinner still to be had with

James and some members of the delivery team and she was not looking forward to that. On second thoughts, she was going to feign some illness and get out of it. She let the head of the delivery team know and he was aghast wondering how they would manage without the salesperson and what they would talk about. One would imagine, going by his reaction, that the only job sales folks did was to keep a conversation running. "I'm sure you will do fine," she assured him. "He's very nice and I have a sneaking feeling he is anyway going with us but just not letting on. Trust my instincts on this; start getting your team ready, this deal is ours. Besides, after a few drinks, all of you will find yourselves to be quite the conversationalists," added Radha with a smile she hoped would take away from any offence her colleague might feel at her words. "Just offer him some single malt from Scotland. He'll feel right at home."

Radha made her way to James to make her apologies. "I'm afraid I must desert you but I don't feel too well. I'm going to take myself off to bed."

"Oh, that's a real pity. I shall miss you."

"That's quite unlikely. I'm usually best in small doses."

*

James entered his room after what he thought was a nightmarish dinner. His jaw hurt from all the false smiling he had to do through dinner. Ordinarily, he never cared for these official meals. They were quite pointless. If it was just his own colleagues, he would have told them so and skipped the meal altogether. But this was a vendor and he did not want to offend them. More so a vendor in another country. He was always wary he would step on some toes or inadvertently commit some cultural faux pas. All the cross-cultural training his office had insisted he take had only served to make him paranoid. So, he hadn't thought to refuse the dinner.

And, if he was to be honest with himself, he had thought dinner was an excuse to spend some more time with the charming Radha Iyer. She was quirky and amusing and never before had he felt like spending more time with someone from a partner team. Or with anyone for that matter. He was a very private person and valued his time alone. Some thought he was aloof but he wasn't. He just liked being alone. It was quite unlike him to have a conversation longer than two sentences with anyone but his closest friends. And there were few of those. This was the first time he had this inexplicable urge to be with someone for longer. Radha was engaging, and while not exactly pretty by any conventional standards, she was easy on the eyes. He had been carried along by the wave of her infectious happiness. She seemed to draw him out of his shell like no one ever had. Really, who could blame him?

He really should stop thinking of some wee chit and go to sleep, James scolded himself. Tomorrow was an early day.

CHAPTER 4

Only let this one teardrop, this Taj Mahal,
glisten spotlessly bright on the cheek of time,
forever and ever.

Rabindranath Tagore

R adha met James at the hotel foyer at 5 am the next morning. It was approximately a four-hour drive from where they were to the Taj Mahal and she didn't want the blistering sun to ruin a magnificent viewing experience. If it got too hot, one would have to run all across the courtyard as the marble would be scorching and one couldn't put their foot down for too long. Nowadays the foot coverings offered some relief from the hot marble when one walked in.

James had read up on the Taj the night before. How the precious stones inlaid in the marble had come from different parts of the world. How the English-style gardens around the Taj were courtesy the British viceroy Lord Curzon under whom the Taj was restored. How it was rumoured, though never established, that those who designed and built the monument were blinded or maimed so that they could not replicate the feat. And what steps conservationists were taking now that the Taj faced the challenge of environmental pollution and acid rain. He had known before that it had been built by the Mughal emperor Shah Jahan, almost four hundred years ago, for his beloved wife Mumtaz Mahal. As monuments of love went, this one was pretty monumental! Though the cynic in James had always wondered how one could say for sure it was built for love. It was quite possible that Shah Jahan was mighty glad to be rid of his wife and the monument was to celebrate his relief at her passing.

He remembered reading the historical fiction series on the Mughals by Alex Rutherford. He had loved the intrigue, the betrayal, the passion that the book portrayed and remembered how Shah Jahan had been imprisoned by his own son, the cruel emperor Aurangazeb, after the latter overthrew Shah Jahan and killed all his siblings including the rightful heir, Dara Shikoh. From enduring love to fratricide, these Mughals seemed to have the entire spectrum of emotions covered.

Radha told James an interesting anecdote about an old Bollywood song that talks about a crown being built for love, as 'Taj' meant crown, and another crown being lost for love. The latter being a reference to England's Edward VIII who abdicated the British crown so he could marry the divorcee Wallis Simpson as he could not, as a monarch, marry against the teachings of the church.

James had expected to be under-awed by the much-touted spectacle of the Taj Mahal but found himself astounded by its beauty. His camera never stopped clicking. He was moved by the devotion that would inspire such a beautiful homage. He and Radha found a spot under a tree and sat down a while from where they continued to take in the majesty of the sight in front of them. Radha also pointed out the place in front of the pool that reflected the Taj where countless couples, overwhelmed by the moment, took pictures of themselves and preserved it for posterity. This was the place where people felt their love mirrored in the legendary love a king had for his queen. The vicarious moment could give anyone goosebumps. Radha also told James that many visiting dignitaries also posed there with their spouses and that it had always been a favoured spot for pictures.

"The real graves of Shah Jahan and Mumtaz Mahal lie in a crypt below. There's a narrow staircase that leads to them and they are for viewing only a few days in a year," explained Radha.

"Sounds like something out of a Dan Brown book. I feel like running down those steps like Robert Langdon and leaping into a dangerous yet exciting adventure."

Radha laughed and told James that the next time he was in India, he should visit Fatehpur Sikri if he had the time. "It is a beautiful city used briefly as a capital by one of the Mughal kings, Akbar. He built a dargah there to honour the Chisti Saint Salim who had predicted the birth of Akbar's son, Jehangir. It really is a beautiful place with its red sandstone. Though I was petrified of it as a child as my mean father spun me some make-believe story of it being washed in blood twice every day and it was layer after layer of blood that gave it the colour. It is rumoured to be built on an old Jain religious site. That's the thing about having a hoary past like India. Whole civilizations lie below the ground we walk on."

The two of them dozed off on the way back to Delhi and when they reached the hotel, decided to meet for dinner at the hotel restaurant after they were changed and a little rested.

*

An hour or so later, they were engaged in quiet conversation over a simple meal.

"You must be quite used to Indian food staying in London," said Radha. "We Indians have finally had our revenge and are now all over your country and paying you back in full measure for your occupation of our land," she laughed. "Soon the only food you will know will be chicken tikka and the only art form you are familiar with will be Bollywood dances."

"I am not rising to your bait," James wagged a finger at her. "You can hardly hold me responsible for what someone else did."

"Not at all," said Radha quickly. "I quite like the British as does most of my family. In fact, a mad uncle of mine actually wrote to your Queen asking her to take back rule of our country as he was disillusioned with our politicians," she chuckled. "So, no hard feelings about a time well past. Some good must have come of it, I am sure. Let's try some continental food. You must be homesick for good old mashed potatoes and shepherd's pie. I've decided to spare you the kebabs, dear *nabob*."

"Don't *nabob* me. I'd have to loot your wealth and tie you to a life of servitude to qualify as a *nabob*."

"It's more an attitude, being a *nabob*," countered Radha.

"Are you saying I have attitude?"

"I'm afraid I am. Though I mean that in the best possible way. There's that whole stiff British upper lip air about you. And I feel I can say this to you now—when I first met you at work, I thought you were quite snobbish. Walking around with a decidedly superior air and giving off the feeling that you were suffering lesser mortals like us because you had no other choice. It reminds me of those Mills & Boon heroes. The TDH types."

"I'm going to ignore the fact that you found me arrogant at first in the hope that your opinion has now changed. You are not the first person to find me arrogant. I am much maligned though. I'm just shy and not easily outgoing which gets mistaken for arrogance. And what is TDH?"

"Tall, dark, handsome," came Radha's quick reply. "To that add your supercilious attitude and you are the very epitome of the hero of a romantic novel. Though you are more red than dark!"

"I am just taking solace in the fact that you find me handsome," said James with a crooked smile.

Radha clamped her palm over her mouth. "I do believe this is the strangest conversation I have ever had with a client."

"I'm glad. It would wound me deeply if I felt you flirted with everyone this way."

Radha's eyes flew to James' face. "Good Lord! Is that what I'm doing? I...I..." she stuttered.

"Oh! Please do not stop. I'm enjoying myself rather. Are all Indian girls this outspoken?"

"Most of us, especially in the younger generation, are. We are quite eager to chase our dreams, get out of our homes, be financially independent, dress up, go out, and yes, even flirt with handsome men," winked Radha. "Though it is true that for many women in India it is still a struggle. There is a path you are expected to take. You are supposed to get married and be a good wife and daughter-in-law and sacrifice your desires for the people around you. I have no complaints against women who want to do this, it is a choice that they have every right to make. But I hate that they are deified and any poor girl who voices her wishes is immediately cast as a self-serving vamp."

"But things are changing," continued Radha. "Women are finding their voices. I anyway count myself among the extremely fortunate few. My parents never made me feel there was anything I couldn't do since I was a girl. This whole concept of feminism was exposed to me only when I started working because up until then, it was an alien concept. There was no battle to fight for women as, in my life experience, I was never inferior to anyone or treated differently. I do have my parents, especially my father, to thank for that."

And at this, Radha teared up. James unthinkingly put his palm over hers. "Did you lose him recently?"

Radha was astounded. "Was I so transparent?" she chuckled and quickly recovered herself. "But I usually think only happy thoughts about him. He had these pearls of wisdom he would drop casually and I would scramble to pick them up and store them away to guide me through life. The only advice I never followed was 'mounam kalaka naasthi' which loosely translates to 'silence destroys strife'. I've never been able to follow that. I must speak and fight and rave and rant. I tell myself that everyone needs a Boudicea to inspire them and I must be that to the millions suffering in silence."

"I'm surprised you know of Boudicea," said James.

"Just as you were surprised that I spoke English fluently," mocked Radha. "Dare I add 'condescending' to the other virtues I attributed to you earlier?"

"Oh! Did you provide a list? I just heard handsome and stopped listening. But if you want to sing any further paeans to me, I am all ears."

"You are all bloated head. I don't know about the ears," laughed Radha. "Anyway, we have enough Boudiceas in India like Velu Nachiyar, Kittur Chennamma, Devi Ahilya Bai Holkar and Jhansi ki Rani. I only mentioned Boudicea because I knew you would be unaware of the Indian heroines. So never mind you being surprised we know of Celtic ones here."

"Touche," acknowledged James. "It is true that most of us in the Western world have a world view that centres around us."

"Now you have gone and ruined any chances of my picking a fight with you by being so gracious," pouted Radha. "Should we order some dessert?"

"We could split the tiramisu. I've been quite the greedy goblin over dinner."

"Sorry, but I don't eat eggs and the tiramisu must have them," replied Radha apologetically. "I am told it is most difficult to eat a meal with me. I can be quite annoying."

"I'm sure your considerable charm must make up for the nuisance value. I, for one, would be delighted to dine with you quite often." Radha almost choked on the water she was sipping. She was sure James could hear her heart thump as she clumsily put down her glass of water.

"That was pretty gauche of me," said Radha as the glass clunked down heavily on the table.

"As a left-hander, I take complete offence at that. It's bad enough no devices are made for us, we even struggle with scissors for crying out loud. Our religious texts have the fallen people at God's left and to top it all the word 'gauche' meaning awkward actually means left in French."

"I must apologize," said Radha quickly. "I meant no offence. And truth be told I find lefties incredibly stylish. I hereby take the 'gauche' back from my earlier comment and replace it with a simple 'clumsy'. Am I forgiven?"

"Of course!" grinned James boyishly. "I was merely exaggerating my wounded sentiments for maximum effect and I seem to have succeeded. Anyway, we southpaws have to suffer and adapt so much from the very beginning, that we have developed great mental fortitude to bear the taunts and bullying of the right-handed world."

The dessert arrived and was devoured and soon—too soon it seemed to Radha—it was time to say goodbye. She was leaving the next morning for Bangalore and James had a flight the following morning out of India.

"I hope your trip was fruitful and the team was able to answer any questions that remained. It has been wonderful hosting you and we are really looking forward to hearing back positively from you. We are very keen to win this deal. Alex should be back in office soon but until then if you have any further questions, please do call me at any time."

James smiled sweetly and replied, "You've been a wonderful host and salesperson. We should have our decision very quickly and I will revert at the earliest. Alas, we go in two different directions from here but I do hope we run into each other sometime."

His kind words seem to stab Radha in the heart as she realized that she truly had enjoyed stepping in for Alex in this deal. She felt empty that it was all at end and that she was not going to see James again. She had felt an easy connection with him and though it had only been a few days and he was very difficult to read, quiet and opaque, she still felt like she knew him.

Chapter 5

Breathes there the man, with soul so dead,
Who never to himself hath said,
This is my own, my native land!

Sir Walter Scott

James woke the next morning with a strange feeling of having lost something. Ordinarily, he would have been quite happy to be headed home. Not that he usually disliked the time he spent in India; he had grown quite used to the noise that was this country on his short visits. But home was England and while his heart may not quite have *burned* when his footsteps turned home—poets were just so melodramatic, weren't they?—he still felt a comfort, a oneness with England. This morning, though, he felt like he wanted to stay longer, like he was leaving something behind that he was not quite ready to leave. He did hate the tedium of travel but it should have been better since he was going home. He should not have been feeling so reluctant.

Ah well, best he got out of bed and make use of the day to get some gifts for people back home. What was the name of the store Radha had mentioned? Chumbak? He had written it down somewhere to ensure he didn't forget. Radha had sworn it was all things Indian and would make for great souvenirs. Slightly kitschy and overpriced, she had said, but the expensive part wouldn't matter to him as he would anyway get fleeced if he went out on Delhi streets alone just on account of the colour of his skin. *Cheeky chit! What an outrageous thing to say.* Thinking of her brought a smile to his lips. He had to admit he had never quite enjoyed a business trip as much as he had the last few days and had a sneaking suspicion she was part of the reason.

She was witty and wholesome. Though the last adjective made her sound more like health food rather than a person, he laughed at himself. Speaking to her had exposed him to the aspirations and hopes and viewpoints of a young Indian girl. He had got a sense of a bright new generation, straddling two worlds, bridging the gap between their Indian upbringing and the call of the world. He imagined young women in India, not just Radha, were all trying to find their identity in this duality. Trying to take the best of both and create an identity.

James shook his head and mentally chastised himself. He had spent all of three days with someone and suddenly he was an expert on the psyche of Indian women? And wasn't it time he stopped threatening to get out of bed and actually got out? He ignored the persistent blinking of his phone as he walked around his room and fixed himself an Earl Grey tea. It had to be work and he was determined to ignore messages from work for the next hour at least. Till he got his brain in functioning order or, at the very least, till he had gotten his ablutions out of the way. What was that book that was all the rage? The 4-Hour Workweek! He needed to buy himself a copy.

One had to admit that Indians got their food right, thought James, after a marvellously delicious breakfast. It had to be the tastiest cuisine in the world, even if it called for one to have an iron lining in one's stomach. He looked around the coffee shop and took in the people. Most fit into a template, suited and booted and engaged in serious conversations with others who could only be business associates. Mostly from the IT industry, thought James. Even though Radha had mentioned in passing the previous day how India was so much more than "software" as she had called it laughingly. She had narrated how the word 'software' was used as an umbrella term by cabbies, autorickshaw drivers and just about anybody to describe the occupation of well-heeled, upwardly mobile Indians, especially in Bangalore. Apparently, it mattered not if the person worked in aerospace or embedded systems, but by virtue of them driving into swanky, glass, high-rise buildings with manicured lawns, they were branded as being in 'software'. Her observations about people were always funny, James thought with a smile and then wondered why he had thought of her. Mentally shaking his head, he picked up his phone to check his email.

He stopped while his eyes scanned the text. *Extend the trip? What on earth!* His boss, Mike, had to be kidding him. Apparently, the deal had gotten visibility at the executive management level and there was considerable push to accelerate the launch of this project. Mike himself was coming in the following week to sign and kick off the engagement. In those circumstances, as Mike wrote in his email to James, it made no sense for him to return to England at the moment.

He would now have to reach out to Radha to give her this news and see how he could plan for this coming week. His fingers tripped happily over his phone as he dialled the number that had now become familiar. *Switched off.* Ah well, ideally it should never have been the first call he made, he thought sheepishly, running his fingers through his hair.

James spent the next hour getting his affairs in order. Sending requests to the travel desk to change his travel and stay bookings. He thought he might as well return to Bangalore and spend the next week with the vendor team and get things set for Mike's arrival. He tried Radha again to let her know of the new plans but the phone was still switched off. Of course, she must be flying back to Bangalore, he realized. He'd wait a little longer and then call Alex. Best he got packed and ready to leave and then go on a little Delhi jaunt.

*

Radha and Lakshmi had just finished a meal at Toit. Radha was always amazed at the crowd at this micro-brewery in Indiranagar which had come to be quite popular. This was a Saturday evening, of course, but it was as crowded even during lunch hours on a weekday. Didn't the patrons here hold jobs? They certainly should, if only to be able to afford this kind of eating out on a regular basis. But it seemed like this place was forever full. One would imagine food and alcohol was being doled out free of cost. But she loved Toit; it had a certain vibe. Something that screamed Bangalore. And Radha loved Bangalore. There wasn't a city in the world she would rather live in than Bangalore. Maybe New York, but absolutely nothing else. If someone asked her what exactly she loved about the city, she wouldn't be able to answer. The component parts were there: the weather, the old-world charm of some parts of the city, the laid-back people, the numerous boulevards with the trees on opposite ends of the road growing into each other and forming a canopy through which sunlight dappled onto the roads, the sheer magnitude of parks and green space, the style factor of the entire city. But the sum was somehow greater than all these parts. One just had to stay a little while in the city before they fell in love with it.

"You're awfully quiet. What are you thinking of?" asked Lakshmi.

"This, that and the other. But is it any wonder the world is getting obese? Look at the people here wolfing down food and alcohol like there's no tomorrow."

"*Don't* fat shame!!" cried Lakshmi. "That's the last thing I would have expected from you, Radha."

She rolled her eyes. "Stop with the exaggeration. You know very well I didn't mean it like that."

"You stop wondering about the obesity problems of the world. There are enough gyms close by. It's a wonderful ecosystem that has been put in place. One works out, then one goes and pigs out, often at a place within 100 metres of the gym. The world is in perfect balance. Anyway, tell me all about our James." Lakshmi said as she lazily stretched her legs and lit up her second cigarette.

"Firstly, he is not OUR James," she answered Lakshmi. "And secondly, could you stop with the smoking already? You are going to the grave early with that disgusting habit. Besides, I've taken a flight back just this morning and while I have had my beauty sleep in the afternoon, you are giving me a headache with that smoke."

"Everything gives you a headache from LED lights to music! I thought you said I looked as stylish as Marlene Dietrich when I smoked."

"I'm pretty sure I didn't. Anyway, why do you want to

foul up your breath and stymie any chances of getting some action?"

"I'm never starved of action, but I thank you for your concern," said Lakshmi with an arched eyebrow. "And I'm pretty sure you got that headache from all the cleaning liquids you must have used when you returned from your trip."

Radha smiled sheepishly. Unfortunately, Lakshmi knew her rather well. Whenever Radha returned home from a trip, it would take her the better part of an hour wiping down everything she possessed. The suitcases would be wiped with Dettol water, the wheels washed in running water, appliances would be scrubbed with disinfectant wipes and any toiletry that had touched a hotel surface would be washed clean and dried. It wasn't that Radha liked being this way; she would have much preferred to be less obsessive as life would be far easier. She wondered why others didn't see it was a disease she suffered from, this constant need to be clean. She needed help, not ridicule.

"Cleanliness is next to Godliness," Radha declared pompously.

"Don't be such a nutjob. And don't think I don't know how all your pretensions to cleanliness go out of the window when it comes to Lucifer. You have his drool and his fur all over you and somehow that bothers you not a bit."

Radha turned up her nose and said loftily, "Some things we do for love."

Lakshmi looked aghast at Radha. "So, I comb my hair with your brush and you go ballistic if I don't wash it after, but you are absolutely okay with his fur being completely visible all over your black leggings? Am I to take it you love Lucifer more than me?"

"Was there ever a doubt?" came Radha's unabashed response. "And you can hardly expect me to use something on my hair when it has been through someone else's!"

Lakshmi brought the chair she was rocking on its hind legs back to the ground with a soft *thud*. "I would continue my outrage just to play along but don't think your plans to change the topic have worked, Radha. Tell me about this man who has you going all ga-ga."

"Just because I acknowledge he is tall, dark, gorgeous, well-spoken, muscular, intelligent and funny, does not mean I am going *ga-ga* over him. Not to mention, he's a client, for heaven's sake! And a Britisher. And *way* out of my league. I'm just in awe for some reason. He is a bit distant though, quiet, a man of few words. With his stiff upper lip, wicked humour yet brooding air. What we would jokingly call the strong, silent types. And his IQ must be around 170! The things he takes away from one reading of a document or one discussion is mindboggling. He is easily the cleverest person I have ever met," gushed Radha.

"And you were saying you weren't going ga-ga over him," mocked Lakshmi fondly. "Methinks the lady doth protest too much."

"How clichéd can your expressions be!"

"I'm sorry I'm not the scintillating wit and sparkling conversationalist you might have preferred," shrugged Lakshmi nonchalantly.

"You are never apologetic about yourself. And do let's stop talking about James. We sound like eighth graders discussing the class stud. Hadn't we outgrown this a while ago? Anyway, we are wasting time. He'd be halfway across the world soon, in dreary England where it always rains. I wish him luck in his sunless life," Radha added unreasonably.

"My, my! Look who's throwing a mighty tantrum!" Lakshmi started singing a rough English translation of an old Bollywood song to the same tune as the original. "Saying no-no someone fell in love with him. Deny him she was supposed to, but indeed accept him she did," she sang lustily, very pleased with her musical translation.

"You do know that you sound meaningless and awful," said Radha though she secretly acknowledged that Lakshmi really was marvellous at this nonsensical thing.

"You are just jealous of my musical talents," she said airily.

"There are talents and then there are talents," said Radha as she picked up her phone which had started to ring. It was Alex.

"Hello, you old so-and-so," said Radha affectionately. "How are you holding up? All obsequies done? When are you back?"

"Yes, the obsequies are done but I need to stay a while longer as Amma needs to get some property transactions started off. I'm back only next week. And Radha, that means you will have to be a dear and cover for me for another week with the client."

"Hey, hey, hey! I've won you that deal already and your

precious James Rutherford is on his way back home all happy and fuzzy from all the looking after he got here. What more can I do for you?"

Alex paused before answering. "About that… I just got a call from him. He has cancelled his trip home as Mike is coming here the next weekend. Apparently, James tried to reach you in the morning to tell you of his change of plans but couldn't reach you so he called me. You'll have to help me host him for another week, Radha."

Radha tried to ignore the soaring of her heart and chided Alex. "You can't be serious. I do have my own work, you know. I can't keep traipsing after your James just so you get rich."

"Your uncharitable words are like a stab in my heart, Radha. Is this something you say to a friend of many years? How self-centred you sound! After all we have come to mean to each other, could you not put in the extra effort? You don't have to do much, just sort him out with an office space and check in on him occasionally. Maybe show him the sights and sounds of Bangalore on a couple of evenings. It's hardly too much to ask."

"I'll be the judge of how much to ask it is," said Radha churlishly. "But I'll do it if only to stop your exaggerated claims on our friendship and what it should count for. You've missed your calling. You belong on stage. Anyway, I'm ringing off now. I'm with Lakshmi and she seems to be staring daggers at me for some reason."

"Say hi to her, will you?"

"If you are going to go all moony-eyed over my friends, I suggest you stop wasting my time and call her directly and say 'hi' or whatever the hell you wish," laughed Radha. But she was used to this. Lakshmi's effect on men never paled.

Radha put down her phone and looked questioningly at her friend. Lakshmi's fingers were playing with her glass of water. She had the most beautifully mesmerising fingers which she attributed to playing the piano from childhood. But this was not the time to admire her elegant and beautifully manicured hands. Radha put on a stern expression and said, "Why are you drumming your beautiful fingers against that poor glass? I guess you have your piano teacher to thank for your fingers at least. You can make quite a statement with them."

"I heard what Alex was saying. On an aside, you need to turn down the volume of your phone. Everyone can hear what the other person is saying. But, coming back to Alex's call, don't you see this as a sign from the gods?"

"I haven't the foggiest idea what you are about."

"Oh, please, Radha! You know very well providence has thrown you an opportunity here by delaying James' trip. This can only mean that the stars have aligned for you to make a match."

"I never knew you could be so ridiculous," said Radha. "I meet someone for a few days and you are having me walk down the aisle with him?"

"You know very well I only meant a fling with a handsome Britisher," shrugged Lakshmi. "The marriage dreams are all your own. But you should think about this Freudian thought. It certainly never came from me."

"I'm ignoring you. Can we go now? I believe you have

eaten your way through the rations of this place. Where does all the food you eat go? If I didn't love you so much, I'd absolutely hate you. Most people just have to sniff food to gain weight and you down hillocks of food and remain a waif. Shall I drop you?"

CHAPTER 6

One's destination is never a place,
but a new way of seeing things.

Henry Miller

The next morning was Sunday. Of course, in the Iyer household that mattered not a whit, chuckled Radha as she got out of bed, woken early by the clanging vessels. She often wondered what the family hoped to achieve by waking this early. Her mother made a special brouhaha about being an early riser. In Revati's mind it was a virtue that she slept so little and nobody wanted to point out anything to the contrary to her. It was in everyone's interest to agree with her on most matters. One's mental peace was vastly enhanced.

Radha checked her WhatsApp. It was really time she came good on her promise of not checking WhatsApp for at least 3 hours after she woke. And though she chided herself, she nevertheless continued to check her messages. Her school group was active as always. Apparently, some yesteryear actress had died and that, for some reason, had triggered a tsunami of messages. Radha wondered why news must be declared on social media. Someone died. Someone else got married. Some politician said or did something. Really, didn't most people get newspapers at home or even read the news online? Where was the necessity to post news on social media groups? And with the number of RIPs this poor dead yesteryear actress got, it was unlikely she would get any resting done at all. She'd probably rise from the dead wondering why her name was being called so often.

She scrolled down the screen to check if James had responded. She had sent him a message last evening to check on him and see if there was anything he needed. Courtesy message to a client stuck alone in an alien city on the weekend, she had told herself. He had indeed responded. He had gotten back last night and was planning to rest today and hoped to meet her in office the next day. She responded, noticing he was online.

> Yes, will meet you bright and early in the office. Can I arrange a cab for you?

I'll just get an Uber, please don't bother.

> Are you sure? Because it isn't too much work for me. I'll just have the travel desk arrange one for you. In fact, let me do that. Where are you staying?

At the Leela.

> Very fancy pants! 🐎

Every job has its perks. 👻

> I'm yet to identify one in my job. 😊

You get to meet TDH foreigners. 😎

> Who seem to think no end of themselves. 🙄

Two blue ticks. He had read that, thought Radha and felt like a silly child. And felt even sillier when she looked at the message header and was disappointed James was not typing. She was acting like a giggly school girl! She was just about to fling away the phone when it rang. It was James. She picked up the call too quickly, cursing herself for seeming like such an eager beaver.

*

Radha had a tough time explaining to Revati that afternoon how she came about taking a Brit to eat idlis. That too right after the storm on Twitter where a British professor had called idlis the 'most boring food in the world'. She had reminded James of this when he was trying it out and he had joked that after his poor fellow countryman was trolled, he wouldn't dare confess to Radha even if he didn't like it. Hadn't poor Maria Sharapova been trolled because she hadn't known a legendary Indian batsman? Radha had assured him that she was not to be counted amongst the bullies of Indian netizens who would, by their sheer numbers, shout down anyone who said anything against India, Indian food, Indian cricketers. This had elicited his admission that he indeed had not found idlis matching Radha's rapturous description of them throughout the scooter ride there.

The scooter ride was even more difficult to explain to her mom. When James had called that morning, she told him she was going out to her favourite idli place in all of Bangalore. He had asked to come along to take in the sights and sounds of Bangalore and had agreed to ride pillion on her scooter. James had showered and dressed in a flash. For the life of him, he couldn't imagine what had come over him. Inviting himself just like that. He hadn't given the poor girl a chance because how could she have refused him? But he wasn't going to analyse this. Must he really tie himself up in knots over someone he may never see after a week or so? The person he had become in the last few days was not him at all.

Radha, on her part, had thrown the phone down and rushed around the room trying to get ready. She hadn't questioned her childish excitement at this outing. Not when she had had twenty minutes to get out of home. James had teased Radha when she had handed him a helmet as she picked him up.

"Is that a warning about your riding skills?" James had asked.

"No, just saving you a lot of money. We have very steep fines now for breaking traffic rules and while it might be a novel experience for you to be pulled over by Indian cops, I do not prefer to have the investigation continue to whether I am carrying my license, my insurance, my emission certificate etc. Because you can count on them to continue their investigation till I am found wanting. They hate to let someone go once they flag them down and I am not giving them the satisfaction of fining me. Not that I don't value our traffic police for what they do, but I'd rather not spend more time with them than is necessary."

And so, they had set off, an unlikely pair, on a rickety, noisy scooter called the 'Blue Angel'.

Mahatma Gandhi road is the arterial road in Bangalore's central business district. A broad avenue cutting through the city, it is the quintessence of Bangalore's old-world charm. It used to be called South Parade as it was south of the military parade ground. From state emporia to large banks to vintage eating joints like Ajantha hotel, it is one of the most sought after addresses in Bangalore. Ajantha hotel is a favourite of nearby office-goers. Hot, stuffy and crammed, it still draws in droves of people during lunch hour and during tea-time for the variety of Indian snacks available then. There are bars and restaurants dotting the sides and interiors of MG road and the road continues to be a walking and shopping haven for many Bangaloreans. There are a few palatial homes along the road, the signature of old Bangaloreans who set themselves apart from the nouveau riche in the newer parts of Bangalore. Even though the majesty of the road has been somewhat diminished in recent years by the metro line, it continues to be a favourite haunt for most Bangaloreans. The prettiest sight is the 200-year-old St. Mark's Cathedral at one end of the road. The beautiful colonial cathedral with its domes and Roman arches began as a garrison church for the East India Company. Radha used to accompany Lakshmi to her piano exams that were conducted in this cathedral. Lakshmi insisted Radha come with her. It had become a ritual and Lakshmi had gotten very superstitious about it. She felt Radha was her lucky charm, and while Lakshmi nervously waited for her turn outside the music centre that housed the grand piano, Radha would love to go into the cathedral and see all the memorial plaques of British soldiers put up by their doting and grieving family and friends. It transported her to another world to see British names; one almost forgot that one was in India. She would only very reluctantly leave when Lakshmi dragged her away after her exam was done. They would then pool in money and share a burger at Truffles, a hangout for youngsters on St. Mark's Road.

But her long friendship with Lakshmi and their escapades together was far from Radha's mind as she rode down MG road with her pillion rider towering over her. She became acutely aware of the inquisitive glances thrown her way by the other people on the road. Especially those on the BMTC buses as they had a vantage position from their seats and could look down on them. She tried to divert her mind by engaging James in conversation. "This was my Dad's scooter. He used to call it his Blue Angel. His most preferred means of transport. Given half a chance he would have reached the ends of the earth on this contraption," laughed Radha. "I hope you don't mind the horrible noise it makes, it's just too old to have the quiet hum of superior bikes."

"Oh no, I'm rather enjoying myself," said James into her ear and the completely nonsensical thought that entered Radha's head was that she was glad she had washed her hair the previous day. Really, she was being beyond ridiculous, she smiled to herself, glad that James couldn't see her goofy smile right then.

"This is MG Road, one of the arterial roads of Bangalore's commercial district. Every city in India does have one road called MG Road. After Mahatma Gandhi. You do know of him, of course."

"Yes, even we clueless westerners know about the Mahatma. One of these days, I am going to start taking offence at how little you think we know. In England, we are anyway aware of how Gandhi was the nemesis of our country's hero, Winston Churchill. Devoted as Churchill was to England, Gandhi was ever the thorn in his flesh."

"Warring leaders aside, we are now flying over Bangalore's largest wholesale market of fruit and vegetables. And one of Asia's largest flower markets. It can be quite a sight, to see all the colours splashing against each other up close. But quite crowded, I'm afraid. It is so crowded that many of us, even diehard Bangaloreans, avoid the place like the plague."

"Wow, that must be a sight!" said James graciously. Radha was so caught up in the act of showing him around and so enthusiastic about it that he felt obliged to reciprocate the enthusiasm. This was new for him. Usually, he wasn't so empathetic about others. Not that he was a bad person, but that he wasn't usually tuned in to others and what they were thinking. He was quite oblivious of people around him at most times. He had better watch out, this girl was changing him.

"Nobody can fault you for not playing along with me. You are a sport. And a polite one at that," teased Radha, correctly judging his feigned enthusiasm.

A while later, she stopped her scooter near Brahmin's Café. "The very best idlis in the world!" she announced. "But do not tell my mother I said that. She believes her idlis are unparalleled anywhere in the world."

"Isn't this rather a large crowd," asked James doubtfully looking at the hordes of people standing outside, quite happy not to be offered any seating. The only chair in sight in the eating area was occupied by a man who sat in front of a giant vessel pouring out a greenish-white liquid—which Radha told him was chutney—onto the plates of eager diners.

"The discomfort will be absolutely worth it," said Radha pompously. "But I warn you, the chutney is not cooked, so eat it at your own peril."

Over idlis and coffee, Radha explained to James that this was quite a famous place with many wannabe imitations dotting Bangalore. None of which could touch the original.

"Would you mind terribly if I smoked?" asked James when they were done. Truthfully, he hadn't found the 'idli' as wonderful as she had touted it to be. He had avoided the uncooked accompaniment and so the 'idli' had seemed rather plain and tasteless. He could understand what his compatriot professor had said. He would get to the hotel and order himself eggs.

"If you want to kill yourself, it's no skin off my back, but you should try and quit. It can be done only if you set your mind to it. My father was a chain smoker and one fine day, he just quit cold turkey. He told me that he promised himself as he threw down his last cigarette that he would do anything, even commit heinous crimes, but never smoke another cigarette. Always told a good tale, my father," finished Radha softly.

James looked down into her face taking advantage of her downcast gaze. He pitied the poor sod who married her. He would have to spend a lifetime measuring up to the exacting standards set by her father. Good luck to him in filling those shoes. A cow ambled across the road with never a care for the blaring horns. Radha asked James if he wasn't going to whip out his camera and take photos of the cow half expecting him to do it after having seen many foreigners turn trigger happy on seeing this novelty. James confessed he had done it on the first trip but now knew there was no dearth of cows on Bangalore roads, though he was at a loss to understand why there were so many roaming the streets. Radha had explained that the cows belonged to locals who milked them but generally left them free to roam the streets.

"And is that allowed? To let one's pets roam freely on the

roads?" asked an aghast James.

"We are an extremely free country," laughed Radha. "So free is every individual that they can do what they want with impunity. Even if it impinges on the rights of others and inconveniences them. This is why I am always amused when someone questions freedom in India. I personally think that some of our freedom should be curtailed, especially if our freedom encroaches on other's rights."

"I'll see you tomorrow at work," said Radha when they reached his hotel. "I'll have someone pick you up around 9 am. I'll go in earlier and make sure you have a desk and phone sorted out since you must spend a week here. Alex will kill me if I don't make it comfortable for you."

"Thanks Radha, I really do appreciate your help."

"It's no trouble. I'll have the driver have the reception call your room when he arrives. And I'll make sure he has your mobile number too, just in case. Be good!"

"I'm never anything but."

Chapter 7

Ask not what you can do for your country.
Ask what's for lunch.

Orson Welles

The next morning, Radha was ready and impatiently tapping her feet when Madan ambled in, rubbing his eyes. He was late despite having been explicitly told to come in early. She scolded him in Hindi. She meant to learn Assamese to converse with him but just hadn't gotten down to it. Madan knew a smattering of Kannada but, somehow, they both stuck to Hindi as a lingua franca. Unapologetic as ever, Madan insisted that he had come early. So early that he hadn't found the time to cook his lunch.

Radha knew that meant she had to buy him lunch. He was a master at getting what he wanted without explicitly asking for it, was Madan. The best negotiators were outside conference rooms, and Madan was ample proof of this. Radha waited with barely controlled impatience as he shuffled his feet and took his time to get the car out.

Radha kissed Lucifer, who faithfully saw her off every day at the gate, bye. She made a few calls to get things in order for James and also checked her WhatsApp. It was the usual—people trying to solve world problems like hunger and housing and basic healthcare as they passed time in Bangalore's nightmarish traffic. If only the collective wisdom of armchair discussions on WhatsApp could be pooled, the world would shoot past a century in development and social indices.

She got into an email war with one of her more obnoxious colleagues. Radha wondered for the umpteenth time when things might completely change at workplaces. As of now, the way she saw it, an aggressive male worker was a go-getter and a leader but an aggressive female worker was just that. Too aggressive for her own good. It was infuriating how everyone admired a male who took charge, barked out orders, pushed others around, hustled and generally got his way. It was his ticket to a meteoric rise within the organization. But should a woman try the same, immediately there was resentment that the woman was overstepping her boundaries and was over-smart. Hopefully with more and more women in leadership positions, this would gradually change but it looked a distant dream as of now.

She stepped into office with an unexpected spring in her step, wondering if the mysterious James was the reason her Monday blues had not made an appearance today. Lakshmi was really beginning to get under her skin! She made the necessary arrangements for James with the facilities in charge and having reassured herself that Alex would have no complaints on how she was treating his client, she got down to work. It was almost lunchtime before she realized how late it was and decided to check on James, something she meant to do but had slipped her mind. She wandered over to his desk and her heart did a funny flip when he looked up and gave her his boyish smile.

"I thought you had deserted me," said James with mock despair.

"You were hardly in the middle of the Sahara Desert so you can ease off on the hyperbole. How's the day been? Have you been able to get any work done? And I hope you've been comfortable?"

"Oh yes, every now and then someone checks on me. I am feeling completely spoilt. I could get used to this."

"Well, I'm glad we haven't been remiss. Alex would have my hide if he felt we did not spoil you silly."

"I was rather hoping this had everything to do with me and nothing to do with the sword Alex seems to be having hanging over your head."

"Don't be silly!" said Radha unable to stop the blush deepening on her cheeks.

"That's a becoming shade you have turned."

"What about lunch?" blurted Radha, changing the topic. "Can I buy you lunch outside, if you have the time? I can continue to give you a Bangalore darshan."

"What's *darshan*?"

"Something like a viewing. You must forgive us Indians. We often speak English mixed with any number of Indian words."

"No, it's nice to learn new words. And, anyway, isn't that what defines English? The influence of so many other languages have contributed to its lexicon. So where are you taking me on the…*darshan*?" James charmingly mispronounced the last word.

"Since it's only lunch and we don't have much time, I'm thinking an open-air restaurant which also has the drive-in option. Nestled in the heart of Bangalore's beautiful Lavelle Road."

"You sound like a tour guide. Does the place have a name?"

"It's called Airlines, and it's beautiful. Green space right bang in the middle of Bangalore's commercial district. Food is pretty simple but the atmosphere is very old-Bangalore."

"Sounds lovely. When do we leave?"

"Right away," said Radha. "Just let me grab my wallet and I'll meet you at the office reception in 10 minutes."

*

James took in the restaurant they were seated in. It was really quite charming, he had to admit. The entire restaurant was under the shade of an ancient Banyan tree whose prop roots from the branches grew vertically downwards creating a visual spectacle for the diners. Everything had a lazy air. There were two gangs of middle-aged men. With their pot bellies and hearty laughs, the two were almost indistinguishable from each other. James wondered aloud how they seemed so relaxed on a Monday afternoon to which Radha replied that the day of the week made no difference to them. They were probably in the real estate or construction business or had some factories running in the outskirts of Bangalore. They were the type that didn't work for money; money worked for them. And they believed in living life to the fullest—taking a leisurely lunch, catching up with friends—living life at the slow pace that had made Bangalore a paradise. Even the waiting staff was laid back. Ambling along in no hurry to serve the clients. Radha had to gesticulate wildly before she finally got someone's attention.

Radha spoke about the people of Bangalore being non-confrontational and difficult to rile. Carrying tolerance so far as to even take traffic and garbage woes with a 'swalpa adjust maadi' attitude, an ability to adjust to any inconvenience.

James laughed and watched Radha's animated face as she continued to speak about Bangalore. Moving from its people to what one could do there. Explaining that there really wasn't much sight-seeing to do be done. Bangalore was experienced, and loved, through its vibe. About how the undeniable charm of the city had turned out to be its nightmare. There had been a real explosion of people who came in from all over the country, began to love the city, and didn't want to return, making Bangalore lose its beautiful green cover as the authorities didn't seem to know how to handle the population growth. And how, apart from being the pub capital of India, it was now also the food capital of the country.

"And where must I go to partake of these delicacies?" asked James.

"Lots of places. Every street will have locals from various parts of India set up little mobile stalls selling everything from momos to Kolkatta kaathi rolls to pani puri. But one needs the constitution of a horse to stomach these foods. If I must pick my favourites, there's the street food of VV Puram, Bangalore and its vibe at its best. And something very unique is the DC canteen; it's a regular canteen at the Commissioner's office complex. I had a lawyer friend who used to drag me there for rushed lunches as the place is quite close to the civil court. They serve the most amazing bread toast with banana jelly. The crowd there is unbelievable, and you will really respect the staff for how they keep the crowds moving with their efficient service."

"You should take me."

"Your stomach may not survive the ordeal. Besides, I don't guarantee you that you will not suffocate. People are packed in like sardines."

"And yet, somehow, you have survived."

"I'm from the third world. We are built to survive crowded places and eat unhygienic food. Shall I check in on you before I leave work in the evening?"

"Why don't you just install one of those baby monitors near my office and check on me through the regular feeds?"

"Now there's a tempting thought!"

"I'm guessing I should feel violated but, for some reason, I'm just flattered."

Radha hurried out with a quick bye and without acknowledging his comment. She had clearly gone stark raving mad. What was she thinking speaking to a client like this? But that he was such a sport must count for something, she tried to convince herself.

CHAPTER 8

En vazhi, thani vazhi
(My way is absolutely unique)

Rajnikanth, Indian movie superstar

James was at work till late that evening and when he headed back in the back of a rather worn-down call-taxi he had booked through an app, he took in the calm of the Bangalore night. The noise and activity of the daytime seemed to have disappeared like a mirage introducing him to a city that seemed alien to the one he was used to. It was beautiful. He realized he had never been out this late in his previous visits to Bangalore and this must be the old-Bangalore-charm everyone spoke about. Especially Radha. She had waxed eloquent on the city of yore. Its quiet roads, its green cover, its lazy charm. Apparently, unknown to many, that Bangalore still resurfaced after everyone had gone to sleep.

James turned in after a quick dinner but was unable to sleep. Random thoughts flashed through his mind. He thought of the lunch he'd had and how he had eaten the spicy food out of politeness. Radha kept checking on him if the food was to his taste but he hadn't had the heart to tell her it was a bit too pungent for his liking. Even if it meant he had to put up with his stomach's protests all through the evening. She seemed so anxious to make sure he could handle Indian food that a perverse part of him didn't want to give in to the stereotype that an Englishman could not handle the food in the subcontinent. Hopefully, he would not have to pay the price for his pride.

He did eventually nod off but had the weirdest of dreams with him running through what seemed to be the park Radha had pointed out in the afternoon, somehow afraid, looking for someone as a drowning man would clutch at a straw. As though finding that person would make his fears go away. When he woke, the dream seemed so vivid that it took a few minutes to get his breathing back to normal. Served him right for experimenting with food. His stomach had escaped the consequences of his pride but the too-strong flavours seemed to have gone directly to his head. Still, it was a break from the usual dreams that tormented him. From the time he was a child, James had had nightmares about snakes. On many nights, he would wake up screaming and thrashing after being chased by snakes in his dreams. The dreams were so real that he would shake out his blankets and check under the bed if a snake was waiting to strike him. This was an improvement. He was still running, but at least not from snakes.

*

By the time Radha came in to check on him the next day, James had already drawn up the project plan and launch details and shared a draft with Mike. He was very respected by his co-workers. There was good reason for this. He had a deep knowledge about his field of work, he was efficient, his planning and analysis were detailed, but most importantly, he could foresee possible glitches and quickly come up with alternate plans. In his younger days, he had suffered a little performance punishment for his quality work. More and more work had been dumped on him just because he was the best at it. But as he had matured as a working professional, he had started putting his foot down, learning to say no, delegating and mentoring others to take on more. He had also learned to go a little easier on himself and not be so exacting in his expectations of himself.

He was deeply engrossed in his work when Radha's mild perfume alerted him to her arrival even before he saw her or she said a word. Mentally groaning at himself, he turned around and wished her a very good morning.

If he told her that he knew the scent of her perfume, what would she say, James wondered with a smile. It would be lovely to see that bewildered, slightly self-conscious expression on her face. But as nice as it would be to see a warm blush spread across her cheeks, he decided to spare her.

"You look awfully chipper for this early in the morning," said Radha as she greeted him back. "What's with the mysterious smile?"

"It's the smile that goes with pleasant thoughts."

"Whatever," said Radha as she rolled her eyes.

"What a pithy set down!"

Radha checked with James if there was anything she could help him with. He seemed a little apologetic but asked for her help in getting to the closest eyewear store. Apparently, he had sat on his glares the previous night and needed a pair. Radha was half-tempted to tease him how he couldn't do without sunglasses for a few days but realized that he was from sunless England and probably didn't see as much sun in a month as he would in India in a few days. She offered to take him around lunchtime herself since it was going to be quite difficult to direct him and they could anyway grab lunch at her golf club which was close by. Two birds, one stone. She just had to get a proposal out of the way and would meet him around noon.

At lunchtime, she realized she was in a fix. Her car wasn't with her as Madan needed to run some errands for her mom and she had been so engrossed in working on the sales proposal that she had forgotten to order a cab. Now it was too late and all the cabs that were available would take quite a while to reach the office. She would have to take James in an auto. This was a bad idea, exposing James to the noise and belching smoke of an auto. But he seemed not to mind and even thought it might be fun. Well, if he called blaring horns going off in his ears and exhaust fumes hitting his face, fun, it was his funeral. She had warned him. Anyway, what was Bangalore without its autos?

Fifteen minutes went by and they were still waiting for an auto driver obliging enough to take them where they wanted to go.

"This is now becoming a huge problem," explained Radha. "I usually prefer autos to a cab ride because they can be taken impromptu and one doesn't have to have the tedious discussion with the cab driver where one explains where they are waiting in an exhausting back and forth of *"what can you see? Can you see a bakery? I am right next to the Airtel office. I am right next to Shanti Sagar hotel"*. One can just flag down the closest auto and hop in. Used to be much more convenient but, for some reason, nowadays they don't want to go anywhere at all! I wonder how they are putting food on their tables by just driving around the city and imperiously refusing every ride!"

One auto did slow down and when Radha told him where they wanted to go, he looked at the time then looked into the distance as though he was contemplating deep philosophical thoughts, and then turned back to her and shook his head indicating he would not take her. Radha then angrily said something to him in Kannada to which he replied apologetically and then they exchanged smiles and the auto driver drove off waving them a cheery bye.

"What was that all about?" asked James.

"I was asking him why he did some doctoral level mathematics before he refused us and he said he was just doing a check to see if he had time to drop us and still get back to the show at the movie theatre where Rajnikanth's new movie is playing."

"Who's Rajnikanth?"

"I do believe you will be beaten within an inch of your life if a die-hard fan of Rajnikanth hears you. He is India's biggest superstar. His fan following defies logic and societal strata. Everyone, especially in the South of India, loves him. Including yours truly. He is called 'thalaiva' which means 'leader' and when his movies release, many people try and catch the first show on the first day. Of course, all of them will have to re-watch the movie because there is so much shouting, whistling, whooping, clapping and throwing of coins on the screen that dialogues are missed."

"Throwing coins?" James wasn't sure he had heard right. What could possibly be the motive to chuck coins on a movie screen? Were the actors supposed to materialize from the screen, stoop and pick up the 'rich' tributes?

"We are very enthusiastic people."

"So, this auto bloke would rather waste money watching a movie rather than earn it?" James was clearly flummoxed.

"It's highly unlikely they will ever make as much as they need. They are probably used to wanting. And movies offer a temporary escape from life's problems. This is nothing. Many actually celebrate the star's birthday by getting together and putting up hoardings of him and cutting cake! All of which they pay for themselves!"

"Bollocks!"

Radha laughed. "Firstly, not bollocks. It's the absolute truth. Visit the South of India around December 12th and you will see for yourself. Secondly, I thought only Hugh Grant says bollocks. So, you have the blue eyes of a Bond hero and the lingo of Hugh Grant. Lucky me!"

And then she stammered realizing what she had just said and quickly looked around for another auto. Luckily, one stopped near them and Radha could avoid looking at James' face and seeing his reaction to her unthinking words. James watched Radha exchange quite a few words with the amused auto driver and caught Radha using the word 'gangster' twice. He was feeling warm with her unintended compliment and seeing her shaking her fist at an amused auto driver only served to increase the warmth that was spreading within him.

He tried to fit his long legs into the crammed space behind the auto driver as he clambered in after Radha, who felt like an idiot. She had forgotten his height when she had brilliantly suggested an auto. Nothing to be done now. It was a short ride so James would have to make do. James checked with her if indeed he had heard her say gangster a few times.

"He wants triple the fare. I told him I had no choice but to agree because the whole lot of them were gangsters holding the city to ransom."

"With how endearing you are, it's a little surprising that no one has slit your throat till now."

When they alighted from the auto, the driver, with a grand and exaggerated gesture, handed back some of the money Radha had handed him, then gave her a condescending smile, as if to demonstrate how magnanimous he was in not taking the fare he had said he would take, and drove off with a distinctly superior air. Radha looked after him in disbelief.

"He did come off looking the better person," said James disloyally.

"I'll thank you to not take a rank stranger's side against me."

But Radha loved auto rickshaw drivers. She had long conversations with them and found most of them to be sweet and chivalrous. Once when she had been trying to find an auto after dark in a secluded space and the driver who did turn up asked her for a little extra money, she had walked off saying she would prefer walking to be cheated in this manner. The poor driver had pulled up and asked her to get on at the normal rate as the road was dark and deserted and he didn't want anything happening to Radha pricking his conscience. Radha had ungraciously mentioned that she was skilled in karate and he needn't bother about her. To which the driver had smirked and said her karate would be of little use when five people were holding her down. She would always remember getting her well-deserved comeuppance at the hands of that rickshaw driver.

At the store, James asked for help while Radha looked around. She tried on a few dark glasses herself but couldn't find anything she liked. Somehow, the glasses that looked so nice on the fantastic-looking models, did nothing for her. There truly was no justice in the world. To make matters worse, as she stepped out of the store, she seemed to miss a step and crumpled to the floor in an inelegant heap. James helped her up and uncharitably laughed.

"Did you just trip over your own feet? Are you hurt?"

She winced. "Only my pride."

James smiled with relief and said, "What next?"

"Next we are again at the mercy of auto drivers. We must proceed to lunch but only when we enjoy the good graces of our temperamental auto drivers."

CHAPTER 9

Have you been flirting with me?
I hadn't noticed it.

Philip Carey (In Somerset Maugham's 'Of Human Bondage')

It was almost seven in the evening when Radha rushed to James' desk to work on the plan of engagement between their two firms.

"Sorry, sorry, sorry!" she apologized to him, hoping that if she said the word many times, it would convey how deeply sorry she was. "The proposal I was working on took much longer than I expected. I had to battle with the finance team to get the pricing I wanted. Convincing them I had the right margins worked out was a hellish task. They were certain I was pushing through some low margin deal just to win it. But it's done now. God's in his heaven and all's right with the world."

"Pippa Passes. Charles Dickens," said James automatically and Radha looked at him in surprise.

"What? I read too," he said with a smile and then went on to assure Radha it was okay she was late as he had anyway not much planned for the evening. They got to work almost immediately. It was well over two hours later that they finished. And it had been two hours fraught with a fair bit of confrontation as each tried to hustle the other to draw up a plan that was most comfortable to their respective organizations.

"I'm glad we are done," said James as he stretched his leg. "I was afraid that one of us would kill the other if we went on for much longer."

Radha caught herself in time staring at his muscled legs and answered, "On the other hand, I have never quite had such a candid and open discussion with a client. I'm usually a lot more polite when I have discussions with them."

"Thank you, I guess? For being preferentially nasty with me."

"No, no," Radha hastened to add. "It's a good thing. Usually, I'm a lot more polite outwardly but I'm actually cursing the client in my mind. And while I was outspoken with you, I find myself bearing you no ill-will at all now. Can I drop you to your hotel? I feel bad having made you wait. My driver had to take off, but I'd be happy to drive you myself."

*

Twenty minutes later and they were still on the road.

"It's unusual to have a traffic build-up this late, right?" asked James. "Even for Bangalore, this must be rare."

"This isn't caused by too much traffic. From the large machines around, my guess is that our water board is doing some work and have dug up the roads."

"Since you have been showing me the sights and sounds of

Bangalore, I guess it was inevitable that we should experience being stuck on the roads of Bangalore together. Otherwise, your guided tour would have been incomplete."

Radha swatted his arm. "Don't bad mouth my Bangalore. I warn you that I will not stand by meekly and allow you to malign the best city in the world."

"I would be bitterly disappointed if you meekly stood by and allowed anything. By the way, is it a little weird that we have gotten this comfortable with each other? I find it quite fantastic at times, when I think about it."

Radha knew what James was saying was true. She didn't want to think about how unnatural it was that she should have become so comfortable with someone in such a short time. With a client. And that too a foreigner. It was unreal. But she didn't want to discuss how unreal, not with him. Leaving it unsaid seemed to do away with the need to explain the situation they were in. Discussing it would mean dissecting it and Radha was having too good a time to spoil it by analysing anything. Too much thought would only destroy what they shared. She tried deflecting the topic with, "Don't tell me you are thinking about me." There it was again. The very devil prompting her to say the most outrageously provocative things to him.

"A lot more than I would care to admit."

Radha flushed and frantically searched for a response when the sound of an impatient horn gave her respite.

"Saved by the bell?" came James' taunt.

"More specifically, the horn," admitted Radha and then looked questioningly through the rear-view mirror at the irate driver behind her. She made a gesture with her hands as if asking the driver behind if she should fly over all the obstacles in her path.

James seemed vastly amused. "You seem ready to pick a fight."

Radha gave him a withering look and replied, "Offence is the best form of defence. Anyway, he deserves it for assuming I was holding up the traffic. Men always assume that women are inept drivers. It's quite frustrating."

Radha and James' attention was caught by a good Samaritan in front who was trying to guide the traffic through the maze of parked earth moving machinery and mounds of dug up mud. He seemed to take his self-appointed role very seriously as he gesticulated wildly, waved frantically and stared angrily at one helpless driver who didn't seem to have the nerve to squeeze through a very narrow stretch.

James looked on amazed. "Why is he scaring that poor driver? It does seem a bit touch and go there with so little space."

Radha laughed. "That's quite common here. A one-inch space is considered more than adequate for someone to squeeze through. And the helpful gentleman there can't fathom why this driver is so reluctant to move forward when he has the luxury of two full inches on either side. Hence the irritation. Thankfully, the driver is a man. If it were a woman, the irritation would have been accompanied by disbelieving looks of *why can't women let someone else drive when they are so hopeless at it* and an accompanying, disapproving shake of their judging heads."

"Sore point?" asked James with a smile.

"Totally! Just watch me overtake a car with a man at the wheel and his Senna-like response will convince you."

Radha and James did eventually manage to get past the blocked area and reach his hotel.

"Do you want to get some dinner?" asked James.

"Thank you, but no! I think I'll head home else my mom will have a search party sent out."

James laughed and they wished each other goodnight.

*

James dragged his feet out of the long shower and towelled himself down. His thoughts remained with Radha as they often had over the last week. But the thoughts were getting more and more persistent. He couldn't fathom why she was beginning to consume him like this. She was not extraordinarily pretty, nor particularly a femme fatale. But he acknowledged that every minute he spent with her was a revelation. Not like quantum mechanics or anything, but more of an insight into a quirky mind. It was quite wonderful that they seemed to be on the perfectly same wavelength. She was really beginning to grow on him. *And if that made her seem like a fungus, so be it*, smiled James to himself.

He lay in bed, unable to sleep for fifteen minutes. Then picked up his phone and turned on his WhatsApp.

Hey, was checking if you got back okay.

It is my town and I did drop you off to make sure you got back okay. But sweet of you to check on me.

Oh! That was poorly done on my part. I got home in one piece. Thank you! Chivalry is not dead 😍

Did you make heart-shaped eyes at me?
Man lives on hope.

And dies in disappointment.

Why aren't you asleep?

I couldn't sleep. Tortured thoughts.

I'm agog. Tell me.

I would, but you'd turn that alluring shade of pink. Which I don't mind at all, actually. But I won't be there to see it.

You are a ridiculous man, Mr Rutherford.

And you are an engaging person, Miss Iyer.

I really should go to bed now.

Coward.

I'll see you only next week as I'm travelling to a client site the rest of the week. I've told Ramesh from our facilities management to keep an eye on you.

Are you an IT company or the KGB?

I shall miss you. Safe trip.

I'll ping you on the weekend to check in on you.

I shall wait with bated breath.

Please don't. I really don't want you suffocating.

You care about my welfare? Dare I hope? Goodnight, Radha.

Goodnight James. Sleep tight. Don't let the bed bugs bite.

Radha looked up and caught her expression in the mirror. She had the goofiest smile ever. She slapped her forehead and threw her head back on the bed. What was she doing? She barely knew this man; he was a business associate and she was flirting with him. And what was even more inexplicable, he was flirting with her. What on earth were the two of them thinking? But Radha prided herself on being a good judge of character and she just knew that James was a good person. Arrogant, opaque, but good. Certainly not the type to kiss and tell. And anyway, they had not kissed.

Now why had she sounded so disappointed by that?

CHAPTER 10

There are as many forms of love as there are moments in time.

Jane Austen (Mansfield Park)

———————

James awoke on Saturday morning with a sense of determination. The last two days at work had been less than perfect as he had missed Radha. In a very short time, he had gotten used to her. He didn't want to analyse why. Their easy rapport was not something he had shared with anyone before. It was not just the good-natured banter but also the moments of companionable silence that were strange. Since answers weren't forthcoming, he decided to go with the flow. He enjoyed her company immensely, and, unless he was reading the signals wrong, she seemed to enjoy his company too. That would have to do for now.

Which brought him back to his sense of determination. He hadn't heard from her over the last three days and he was going to give her till the afternoon or he'd message her. Nothing ever came of sitting around, waiting for things to happen.

*

Radha sipped her special tea as she tried to read the paper.

The morning coffee routine was done, as was the early bath. It didn't matter in the Iyer household if one had anything to do or anywhere to go. One just got up early and bathed and dressed early. *Then* one could sit and twiddle one's thumbs. Long years of this enforced as a rule, had made this a habit for Radha. So, bathed and clothed, she sat down to her heavenly brew of tea and caught the headlines. The paper had all the information that one needed to feel miserable, what with mudslinging politicians, a fickle stock market, the numerous crimes and a less than stellar performance of the Indian cricket team. As far as Radha was concerned, news was highly overrated. She flung the paper down and let her thoughts drift to James, as they had so often in the last two days.

Her fingers were itching to text him but she had held back over the last three days. She didn't want to seem too eager, or worse, too forward. And then, the feminist in her revolted. Why should she wait around like a simpering heroine for the hero to make the first move? She was going to reach out today and propriety be damned. She would finish breakfast and then text him. Her grandmother's dosas were too good to be passed over for a dialogue with a man. Even if the man in question was an Adonis.

A witty Adonis.

A lovable Adonis.

She shook her head at her silliness and attacked her dosa, a savoury pancake, with renewed vigour. Her granny brought out one more crisp dosa.

"No Paati, I'm full. I'll eat this only for greed," said Radha, using the Tamil name for grandmother to address her.

"Nonsense. *Chaapdu*, eat!" said Paati.

"Amma, will you split one with me?" Radha asked Revati. "I'm too full to eat another."

"Then I suggest you eat half and throw the other half. I, for one, am going to eat a full one," said Revati saucily. "I detest this sharing business. Why should I eat lesser just because you want half?"

"You just contradicted yourself. You've always told me never to waste food. What happened to 'waste not, want not'?"

"We both know you aren't going to waste it. You are going to give it to Lucifer who has right now created a little pool of drool near your foot. Put him out of his misery and feed him something, won't you?"

And as though Lucifer understood every word that had been spoken, he made his large, pleading eyes larger and more pleading.

"I swear you understand English as plainly as humans do," scolded Radha. "Your Bambi eyes just got Bambi-er!"

But Lucifer's eyes never wavered a bit from the piece of dosa dangling from Radha's fingers. Radha recollected the story from the Hindu text, The Mahabharatha, where the famed archer, Arjuna, responding to his guru's query on what he saw when he took aim at a bird, answered that he saw only his target's eye. This was in contrast to the answers given by the other archery students all of whom said they saw the tree in which the bird sat, the foliage, the flowers etc. Well, Arjuna would have been proud of Lucifer, thought Radha with a smile. Lucifer could match Arjuna's single-minded focus any day. She threw him the scrap which he caught with the utmost of agility and skill. This dog was a great loss to the sporting world.

Radha picked up the phone and texted James, asking how he was. He was online and she felt needy waiting for his response. But he obliged her and texted back almost immediately berating her for having ignored him for three days and not checking on his well-being. How he went from there to asking her to lunch, James would never know. But it was done. To his relief, she took all of thirty seconds to agree to meet him, even though her response seemed half-hearted, like she was being taken to the guillotine. He teased her about it, professing to be very hurt and wondering if he, as a tall, dark hero—her words, he reminded her—would be meted out this treatment, what would happen to lesser men?

Radha assured him that no man, lesser or greater, had ever evinced any interest in lunching with her and his quick response of "Then the good people of this city must be blind" warmed her heart. He offered to pick her up since he felt she was doing all the work all the time and he was beginning to feel useless. But Radha assured him that they were not in Edwardian England where the lady was fussed over and that he could return the favour when she was visiting England. For now, Alex would kill her if she didn't do things the right way.

"Ah! That motivator of your actions—Alex. I have half a mind to wish him away," James teased. And there was that silly smile on her face again. She was going to have to stop acting like a teenager with a crush! Mentally berating herself, Radha was planning to get on with the day when Lakshmi called.

"Hello, you," Lakshmi's lilting voice drafted over the phone line.

"Hey," said Radha. "What gives? Isn't this a little early for you?"

"You make me sound like some sort of lotus-eater," said Lakshmi. Radha could almost see her pout over the phone. "I'll have you know that I'm as hard-working as anyone else."

"Yes, you are. You just make it look easy."

"Compliments from my greatest critic? You must be in an amazing mood," said Lakshmi, suddenly alert for all the news.

And, of course, Radha told her everything about the previous week.

Lakshmi's disbelieving silence was short. "I hate to say *I told you so...*"

"Who are you kidding? You absolutely love saying that!"

Lakshmi *tut-tutted*. "Be that as it may, Radha! I encouraged you to get into a light office flirtation. You yelled and screamed till you were blue in the face and now I see you have turned this office flirtation into something at an altogether different level."

"Don't be silly," said Radha defensively. "It isn't anything too serious. We just enjoy ribbing each other and enjoy each other's company. Anyway, he goes back after the project kick off and that will be that. He will be just a romantic story I tell the children I have with the uninspiring, but good, stolid man I will eventually marry."

"I suppose you think it is normal for people who have known each other for a little over a week to behave this way with each other?"

"It isn't that uncommon," she shrugged. "And perhaps only I feel the romance. I'm guessing Britishers do this all the time! If I had known I would be subjected to the Spanish Inquisition, I wouldn't have told you anything. I'm not analysing this, Lakshmi. For once, I am going to throw caution to the wind and just do what makes me happy."

"Don't play the ever-suffering victim with me, Radha. You always do what makes you happy. Are you sure you aren't violating any PoSH rules?" asked Lakshmi, suddenly serious.

"I'm pretty sure it counts as harassment only if one of us is unwelcoming of the attention."

"Even so, I think you should keep your HR involved. They might have some policy on office romances."

"It's very premature for that, Lakshmi. And don't worry, okay? It's just a silly flirtation which will blow over in a few days. If it should ever get serious, I promise you I will keep Priya informed."

"Who's Priya?"

"The lady in HR."

"Will you stop using names like I was familiar with all your office colleagues?" said Lakshmi in an irritated tone.

"All right, but don't you think this conversation about James has been done to death? I've told you everything. I feel a strange connection with him and he makes me happy. But right now, it's only that. Some harmless fun with someone I have come to like immensely in a very short time. What's more to tell?"

"And you both haven't yet discussed this with each other?"

"It's more like the elephant in the room. I think both of us don't want to complicate anything by discussing it. We are skirting the fact that our behaviour is uncharacteristic considering the situation we are in, the length of time we have known each other and the obvious short-lived nature of our association. I'm guessing we know it's fleeting and hence not defining it for risk of it being ruined. At least that's true for me. What James is thinking, I can't say for sure."

Lakshmi pondered this for a while and then said. "To quote you from one of the many Jane Austen books you swear by: *Maybe it's not time that determines intimacy. Seven years would be insufficient to make some people acquainted with each other, and seven days are more than enough for others.*"

"I'm touched! You actually pay attention when I quote Jane Austen. This is a blow-air-kisses moment."

"I will literally disown you if you utter even one *muaah.*"

Radha laughed and said, "I'm off to bedeck and bejewel myself. I'm going to lunch with a handsome foreigner," and rung off without giving Lakshmi any further chance to retort and went to find Revati.

"I'm not having lunch at home, Amma. I need to accompany James Rutherford to lunch."

Revati distractedly answered, "Isn't it uncommon for you to spend time with a client on a weekend?"

"Yes, but I just want to err on the side of caution so Alex has no cause for complaint," said Radha and hoped her mother wouldn't probe any further.

"Did you know that cabbage was on the menu today? I half believe you have cooked up this lunch plan after finding out what was for lunch at home."

Radha thought to herself, *Handsome, funny* **and** *saves me from cabbage? He is more my knight in shining armour than I give him credit for.*

Revati shouted after her. "Remember to take the keys and let yourself in. I will not have my siesta disturbed!"

"Will do," said Radha as she raced to her room. It was still early but she wanted to find the right clothes and dress up. She was truly going insane!

CHAPTER 11

Louise, no matter what happens, I'm glad I came with you.

Thelma and Louise

———————

Radha was waiting impatiently for Madan at the gate on Monday. She had told James over lunch on Saturday that Alex was back and he would take over. James had expressed some concerns about the transition being smooth especially since Mike was going to be there, but she had allayed his fears and promised to ensure the handover was smooth.

Madan was late. Only by five minutes, if he was asked, but for the person waiting, even five minutes stretches out interminably. She called him for the fourth time in five minutes since he hadn't picked up. This time he did. Radha barked angrily at him asking if it was too much to expect that he picks up the phone. Madan's calm and perpetually unperturbed voice replied saying he was cycling and could not hear the phone. Radha told herself to take deep, calming breaths. He was infuriating. You'd think he would at least sound the slightest bit apologetic, but he assured her that he was less than two minutes away and Radha was mollified. She sat down on the porch step next to Lucifer and stroked his neck. Lucifer, encouraged by this display of affection, turned his head to the side and gave Radha a long, slurpy lick from wrist to the tip of her fingers.

"Eww, Lucifer!" she said. "Now I'll go to office smelling like a dog."

Lucifer cocked his head to the side and looked puzzledly at her. As if wondering how that could be a bad thing. Smelling like a dog was a perfectly acceptable situation.

"You know the cocked-head, large-eyed routine works on me every time, don't you?" said Radha with a smile. She bent down and kissed his head only to receive the gratifying answering *thud* of his thick tail as he thumped it up and down enthusiastically. Maybe she should skip work and just sit around all day cuddling Lucifer, she thought. But then Alex would kill her if she didn't do a proper handover, and whom was she kidding, she wasn't going to give up the opportunity of spending the day with James. Especially since, now that Alex was back, she wouldn't be spending much time with him. At the thought, Radha felt an unfamiliar pang in her heart. She was being silly. Of course, he would go away eventually; she had always known that.

Madan sauntered in and picked up the keys. She asked him how he always managed to be late when she was on time to which he replied unfazed that since there were very few occasions Radha was ready before he arrived, they stood out in her mind. Radha would have liked to take a stick and beat him. Equality was highly over-rated. If they returned to feudal times, it would serve impertinent Madan right.

Shouting her *byes* to Revati and Paati, Radha got into the car. She had to make a couple of calls to remind some folks that they were needed for the handover meeting, which she did and after answering some of their questions, she hung up. As usual, everyone had saved their questions for the last minute so she was almost half way to the office by the time she finished her calls. One could criticize Bangalore traffic all one wanted, but it sure helped in getting phone conversations out of the way before work started!

Her WhatsApp alert was telling her she had unread messages so she opened the application expecting to be completely entertained. She wasn't disappointed. The topic of the day was the ruinous state of underwear sported by some of the boys in her school group. The topic had caused one of the more genteel members of the group to leave. Radha jumped in and told the usual suspects that their threadbare unmentionables was not a topic of interest to anyone. Only to be teased terribly for her civilized word for underwear and then to be assured that the genteel folks who left would certainly return as nobody could stay away from them for long. Radha did see their point. Everyone seemed to have a masochistic tendency of returning to the mayhem of this group.

*

Radha went up the office entrance steps two at a time. She was eager to meet Alex. She had missed him when he was away. He was her only true friend at work and she was glad he was back. She called him to check where he was and he responded that he and James had gotten in early and were in the conference room, catching up with each other before the others came in. Since there was still some time left for the meeting to start, it was just the two of them.

"Okay. I will be there in a jiffy. Right after I powder my nose."

Radha reached the conference room a few minutes later and rushed to Alex to hug him.

"Welcome back! I've missed you. How's everything at home? Is aunty okay?"

Alex loosened his bear hug and said, "You are a sight for sore eyes! Yes, we are all well. And in the true spirit of the circle of life and death, in the midst of granny's obsequies, my cousin delivered a baby girl. Guess what I recommended naming her? Radha."

Radha shoved at Alex's chest and said disbelievingly, "No!"

"You are not a bad ideal to aspire to. I personally would be quite happy if she turned out like you. I hope she can also seamlessly bridge both the modern and the traditional worlds, like you do."

"You must really have missed me. You are talking rot!" said an embarrassed Radha. She had never been great at accepting compliments. "And…seriously? 'Seamlessly bridge'?? You have clearly been in the IT industry for too long. Next you will be framing full sentences by merely throwing together terms like neutrality, actionable analytics, Industry 4.0 and paradigm shifts in various permutations and combinations."

"Very funny. Seriously though, thanks for managing everything when I was away. James was all praise for you."

And then both Radha and Alex suddenly realized that James was still in the room and turned to look at him only to see him watching them with a bemused air. Alex mumbled his apologies but James interrupted him by holding up both his palms and saying graciously, "Don't mind me. I'll just clear some emails before the meeting starts," and turned his attention to his laptop.

By this time, though, the rest of the folks required to be attending this meeting had started trickling in and introductions were made. The early birds swapped chairs so they had the more comfortable ones and adjusted the heights of their seats to their comfort. There was a lot of shuffling of feet, bags being unzipped, laptops being opened and the usual rush to find charging points for laptops and phones. Radha went up to the laggards who had still not sent their presentations. Those who seemed to think a dramatic photo finish in sending material at the last minute made for a good climax in an otherwise dull office scenario. At Radha's fevered exhortation to send the presentations across at once, they made a show of rushing but, of course, the connectivity was poor in this particular conference room and the presentations were inexplicably large files so the emails took some time in reaching her. The corporate workplace was certainly a great way to test one's patience. Finally, she had all she needed and she put up the agenda slide and adjusted the resolution till she had a clear image.

Just then, as if on cue, Mike walked in and introductions were made yet again and cards were exchanged.

The morning session went off to Radha's satisfaction. There were, of course, the usual, unavoidable gaffes. Like the overenthusiastic person from delivery who droned on and on, with not a care if the audience was still engaged. Radha felt for the poor fellow. One couldn't really blame him; he was absolutely enthralled by his own work. Nevertheless, she and Alex had to contrive to get him to stop talking before they completely lost the audience to boredom.

Then there was the other greenhorn from the marketing team. He would always find the need to mention things that would lead to further questions from the client. He would then sit back, rather pleased with his own contribution to the discussion, completely unaware of the Pandora's box he had opened. The brunt of all ensuing questions would then be borne by poor Radha and Alex who would valiantly try and steer the discussion back to more familiar ground. But despite these minor hiccups, Radha felt the meeting went well. Mike looked like he wasn't yet regretting giving them the deal, which was as good a start as any.

Lunch was announced and passed by as all corporate lunches did—with small talk, discussions on the global economy, enlightened recommendations on public policy of one nation state versus another and a few laughs courtesy some noteworthy global political leaders who had no idea how funny they were without actually meaning to be so. James and Radha, whose personal kinship was not known to the others, shared a few secret smiles during the meal, especially when the topics touched on conversations they had already had.

Soon after lunch, Alex found Radha alone for a moment and quizzed her. "What's with you and James?"

"Excuse me?" said Radha but mentally cursed Alex for being so perceptive.

"Drop the innocent act, Radha! You know exactly what I mean. I sensed a connection and the two of you kept smiling at each other as though you were in on some secret joke."

"Don't be absolutely ridiculous, Alex!"

"Say what you want, but I haven't seen any brilliant smile

directed at me in all these years. And yet you were bestowing them on him throughout the lunch."

"And in all these years, I have never heard you call my smile brilliant. Be still my beating heart!"

"That's because you never directed any dazzling smile at me," said Alex with a glare.

"And we are back where we started," said Radha crossing her hands across her chest. "We could do this forever."

Alex wagged a finger at her and warned her this discussion was far from over. Radha, happy to be let off the hook for the moment, winked at him and made her escape. Having satisfied herself that things were going to plan and Alex was fully in the know of things, she made her exit from the meeting in the next *bio break*—how Radha hated that euphemism used by corporate India. She found James briefly and told him she would catch up with him later that evening or the next day and assuring Alex she was just a call away, she went back to her desk.

She had fallen behind on some of her work. Work that had deadlines was getting done despite the extra workload of managing Alex's James. So, proposals were getting sent, RFPs were getting responded to and client queries were getting answered. But some of the new things she wanted to try had fallen by the wayside and she needed to pull up her socks. Later she would dwell on the news Alex had given her about James staying back a while. Obviously, she was thrilled to hear that. Even if she wasn't going to be running into him often. For now, she needed to focus.

*

"You haven't left," stated Radha rather stupidly later in the day when she went to meet Alex and noticed that James was still there.

"Actually, I have. This is just a hologram I left behind to keep Alex company."

They all laughed but Radha could see from the corner of her eyes that Alex was staring strangely at her as if to ask since when she and James had gotten so chummy. She deliberately ignored him and said to James, "So, we have started off on the right foot? I wish you all luck!"

"Why does that sound like a goodbye?" asked James.

"It isn't really. But it's not likely we will run into each other much from here on so just thought I'd wish you luck."

We'll see about that, James thought but loudly only said, "Thank you. You've been a huge part of the reason everything has gone off well so far. And you've been most hospitable. My deepest thanks. The tough part starts now. Alex will have his hands full."

They both turned to Alex who was looking, in turn, at each of them, his mouth a little open.

"You look like you are watching a tennis match, Alex," teased Radha.

"Sorry. It's just that I was thinking you have charmed my client so much that I'm not sure I'll measure up to the task of taking up from where you've left off."

"She will be a tough act to follow," said James fondly.

Radha mentally cursed him. Alex would subject her to

third degree questioning for this. She quickly attempted to change the subject with, "Well, it's largely up to the delivery folks now. Even the moron Alex won't be able to mess it up."

Alex stared daggers at her as they all walked towards the exit. At one point, when James was ahead, he whispered to Radha, "You have a lot of questions to answer, my friend. I'm not letting you off the hook." Radha laughed dismissively pretending to be a lot braver than she actually felt. Alex was like a hound on a scent trail. It wouldn't be easy to shake him off.

Chapter 12

*I am glad it cannot happen twice, the fever of first love. For it is a
fever, and a burden, too,
whatever the poets may say.*

Daphne du Maurier (Rebecca)

The next two months passed pretty quickly for Radha. Work was busy and the passing days blurred into each other in such a manner that it was difficult to keep track of the passage of time. Some weeks, it felt that it went from Monday to Friday in the blink of an eye. She did run into James at work but the excuses to meet were no longer there and it seemed each of them was reluctant to go out of their way to create a situation where they met. Nevertheless, they did run into each other and, on all those occasions, Radha was relieved to note, their easy camaraderie was not lost. Alex had given up on questioning her, having accepted there was not much point in continuing his sleuthing. Radha thought that mostly stemmed from Alex realizing she was uncomfortable answering his questions. And Alex was nothing, if not thoughtful and empathetic.

James, Radha had come to figure, believed completely in living life on his terms. He continued being funny and provocative and teasing with Radha irrespective of Alex's presence. And, when the entire team had gone out together after work on a couple of occasions and Alex had asked her to tag along, James had been quite partial in his attentions to Radha, rarely sitting elsewhere and always conversing with her for the larger part of the evenings. Radha was sure the others might be thinking it strange but they all had the good sense to pretend to ignore it. Plus, she was friends with Alex. Nobody wanted to mess with someone who was a 6'2" colossus. Besides, Alex was much admired, and, because of her association with him, Radha seemed to have escaped the worst of the office gossip.

Radha did think, quite often, about the whirlwind two weeks she had spent with James when she was standing in for Alex. They were happy times and, almost always, Radha smiled to herself when she recollected her conversations with James, his teasing humour, her sometimes unthinking statements and his unfailing response in taking on those very same statements and embarrassing her. She missed the time spent with him, if someone could miss something one had for such a brief period of time. But she also liked this phase when he was still around and they still ran into each other. The fleetingness of the time devoted to him had now morphed into something more substantial. While she had viewed the time they initially spent together with much excitement, the shadow of it being temporary had always made it seem unreal. Now that they remained in touch, their relationship had become more comfortable, more realistic and more grounded. They did text each other quite often and the silliness with him that she had come to love, continued. As if thinking of him had conjured him up, Radha saw her mobile beep with his message.

'Sup?

I thought only twelve-year-olds said that.

As opposed to me who is sixty?

Busy?

Nope. Wiling away my time. Twiddling my thumbs. You get the drift.

So, wanted to check with you. My friend wants something for his wife. Any suggestions?

You can get a stole. There are some very pretty silk ones you could pick up. Very bright and vibrant. Very 'India'. I'll send you the store locations of a few places that have good stuff.

Okay thanks. And how's the mega proposal you were working on coming along?

It's okay. But we aren't going to get that one, I'm fairly sure. The incumbent is strong and hasn't really messed up. It's going to be difficult to dislodge them, especially considering the goodwill they have with the client. I think the RFP process might be a farce.

So, you aren't really responding?

We are! Man lives on hope. Besides, no matter what,
we still have to put our best foot forward.
A salesperson lives on the hope that
the future is always bright.

Seems futile.

Yes, but the basis of my upbringing is to do one's duty
irrespective of the outcome. It's in our Bhagavad Gita.

I'm aware of the Bhagavad Gita.

Well done. More and more I am convinced you aren't as
clueless as I thought you to be.

And, more and more I am convinced that your waspish
tongue ill recommends you.

Sue me, if you must.

There is no way I am messing with someone
with such litigious genes.

Huh?

Didn't you say your great grandfather sued some
Englishwoman?

Ah! You remembered. Half the time I
prattle on with nary a care about who is listening.

I always listen.

Mighty attentive of you.

Of course, you have to have the last word.

And of course, you will try to wrest it from me.

I give up.

Be right back. My mom seems to be bellowing.

Radha shouted to Revati asking her what the problem was and why she was hollering. Revati shouted back in a hurt tone that she was hardly hollering and that that she was only *very* upset that it had started raining just a few hours after she had watered the garden. Radha told her the rain gods were probably trying to vex her on purpose. But Radha's sarcasm was completely lost on Revati who heartily agreed and added the weather to the entire battalion of people and elements who were out to get her. Radha asked if she could have a moment's peace, and hearing no response from her mother but a wounded silence, she was just going to go back to chatting with James when her phone rang. It was Lakshmi.

Why did everyone think of her at the most ill-timed moments?

"Hello," said Radha gruffly.

"What happened to you? Why are you in this sunny mood?" said Lakshmi, never one to be dissuaded by subtle hints.

"Was chatting with James and, first Amma, and now you insist on talking to me."

"Is this how you treat your friend of many years? Throw her over for some Johnny-come-lately? Or in this case, a James-come-lately."

"Was there a reason you called?" asked Radha wearily.

"Nope. I just called to chat but it doesn't take an IIT

graduate to see my call is not welcome."

"What on earth does a graduate of one of the Indian Institutes of Technology have to do with this conversation?" said Radha rubbing her head with her fingers. The irony of it was that one actually chose one's friends. So, really, she had no one to blame but herself that this pest was her bestie.

She knew what Lakshmi meant, of course. In India, admission to the IITs was the pinnacle of tests to prove one's intelligence. There was no higher testimony to one's IQ than if one was from IIT. It was a lifelong badge of honour in India. Forever after, the parents of those who were admitted would say, 'my son/daughter is from IIT'. This was Lakshmi's rather long-winded way of saying she got the hint that her call was not welcome even if she wasn't as smart as an IITian.

"Heaven forbid I keep you from your precious James. I only called to ask you to see the video I sent on WhatsApp."

"I did," said Radha. "I even sent the thumbs up emoji because I liked it."

"Liar! That's why I called. To tell you I'm onto you. The video was five minutes long and you sent your false emoji thirty seconds after you saw the message. Who are you kidding?"

Radha realized she had been caught red-handed but there was no backing down with Lakshmi. If she sensed any weakness she would swoop down on Radha like a peregrine falcon. Instead, she took her on with, "You need to get a life! Checking the info tab on WhatsApp to see who read your message and when. Don't you have anything better to do?"

"If I did, would I be calling on this trifling matter? Hey, my paper on *Inherent Sustainability of Ancient Indian Architecture* was selected. I'm off to Brazil to present it in four months."

"That's fantastic!" Radha was ecstatic. Lakshmi had been very excited about this paper. Her last two papers hadn't been selected and she had pinned her hopes on this one. She had even made Radha read it though she hadn't understood a word. "I told you it was great!"

"Lying again!" said Lakshmi. "You told me you went to sleep reading it."

"That I did. But that's only because I lacked the intellect to comprehend it. But I did tell you it would get accepted this time."

"That you did. Anyway, you run along to your James. A girl knows when she is not wanted. I'll talk to you later. Treating you to lunch one of these days."

"Okay. See you soon," said Radha and hung up. She quickly went back to WhatsApp hoping James was still online. Her heart soared to see he was.

> Sorry, where were we?

I was left waiting while you went to check on your mother. Never mind that. What plans for today?

> Not much, planning on watching a movie re-run.

Anything I might know?

Unlikely. One of our typical Bollywood movies. Some period drama with the usual ingredients. Billowing tapestry, opulent chandeliers, larger than life visuals, a riotous burst of colours, an impossibly beautiful woman holding her impossibly beautiful hips at impossibly seductive angles while her limpid eyes and unshed tears give us a peek into her unspoken grief.

If you are going to be nasty about it, why watch it?

It's fun to watch and ridicule.

To each his own mode of entertainment.

Or hers.

Forgive me—his or her own mode of entertainment.

So, Alex tells me you will be headed back to England soon?

Yes, I might need to come back in a few months, but for now my job here is done. I should be able to manage remotely for the next phase.

You must be looking forward to going home! You've been away too long.

Yes, I am. I do miss England but I've grown to love Bangalore as well. The weather is quite like England.

Which is why your compatriots preferred Bangalore even in the days of our occupation.

The weather is just one factor. I've come here
a few times before and have always liked the place.
But this time was a lot longer than the previous
visits and I've really taken to it.

Well, I'm happy my city meets your exacting standards!

There were a few other factors also this time.

Dare I ask what?

Only if you have the courage to hear the answer.

I am the most cowardly person I know 😅 🏃

I'll spare you then. But suffice to say the other factor
played a very significant role in my enjoying this trip.
I'm almost sad to be gone. I shall miss these days.

And you shall be sorely missed too.

That's more than I've ever got, so I'm going to quit when
I am ahead. Ciao then.

Bye, James.

Two simple words, thought James as he put his phone down. *Bye, James.* But why did *James* sound so nice when she said it. He could swear that he had never liked his name more than when he heard it from Radha. The past two months had been a little like the opening lines of Dickens' Tale of Two Cities. It was the best of times. It was the worst of times. The best parts had been when Radha and he had been thrown together by circumstances. They were still incredibly comfortable in each other's presence. That never stopped surprising him, more so because they saw much lesser of each other now. He would have thought they would have gotten awkward but each time they met, it was like they just picked up from where they left off the last time. Even if the last time would have been a week ago. It was almost as if they had a connection that never weakened. The worst of times was when days went by without seeing her or talking to her. Working hours were bearable since his mind was occupied with the significant amount of work that needed to be done. But apart from that, he missed her. It was difficult to fathom how he had gotten accustomed to having her around in such a short time. But he had. Curse his cowardice that he could never muster up the courage to go up to her without any reason. He always stopped short of obviously courting her.

He wasn't sure why this was. Was it because she was Indian? Was it because they shared a workplace? Was it because he was afraid that he might frighten her off and lose the easy relationship they shared? He could never tell, though he wrestled with these questions quite often. When he was unbearably eager to talk to her, he would make up some silly excuse like the one he had today. *His friend needed something for his wife?!* How lame was that?

I'm really pathetic, thought James as he helplessly ran his hand through his hair. He was going insane and the only silver lining was that he would be home soon and this madness would be behind him. He would make sure he swept right half a dozen times after registering himself on Tinder. And for good measure on Bumble too!

CHAPTER *13*

Absence makes the heart grow fonder.

Thomas Haynes Bayly

———

Radha had promised to drop James off at the airport when he was leaving. He had sworn it was completely unnecessary and that considering his flight left in the wee hours of the morning, it would be quite inconvenient for her. He was worried if it would be safe for her to travel back alone in the night but she had assured him that since the office was anyway arranging his drop off, it would be one of the regular drivers and absolutely safe. Besides, she took late flights back into Bangalore all the time so she was quite used to it. James had agreed largely because he had been insanely glad that she was taking the trouble for him. That should count for something, he told himself.

Radha, on her part, had the toughest time explaining to Alex why she was going. He had raved about how bad it would make him look as, ideally, if someone had to accompany James, it should have been him. To which Radha had responded by assuring him that there was no protocol involved as there was absolutely nothing official about this. Alex teased Radha that she sounded like the Pepsi advertisement from the Cricket World Cup many years ago but gave in. Mostly because he loathed inconveniencing himself more than was necessary.

And so it happened that Radha accompanied James to the airport the night he was leaving. Strangely, the ride to the airport had been very quiet. Gone was the teasing, the flirting, the easy back and forth that had become the recurrent theme in their conversations. It was as if the finality of their situation had hit the two. The conversation was stilted. The air between them strained. Radha began to wonder if this had been such a great idea. The last thing she wanted was for their association to end on an uncomfortable note. She wanted to kick herself for this hare-brained scheme. But, in her defence, she hadn't for a moment imagined that they would both pick this time to go quiet and uncomfortable. Both made a few feeble attempts to rediscover the connection but then gave up and rode the rest of the distance in silence.

When they took the ramp up the airport, James said, "Sorry, I've been poor company. I hate flights and I'm usually quite a sullen bear in the hours leading up to a journey."

"Don't bother," said Radha gamely. "I've been pretty poor company myself."

They alighted from the taxi and after Radha told the driver where she would find him, they walked up to the front of the airport.

James said, "I'm early. Do you want to get some coffee?"

"Sure," said Radha determined to draw out their time together now that it had dawned anew on her that their association was almost at end. They picked up their beverages and found a quiet corner.

"So, this is it," said James with an elegant shrug of his broad shoulders.

"Yes, it is," answered Radha rather unnecessarily. She was feeling ridiculous. Why must she be so sad and mopey now? She had hoped to dazzle him one last time and give him something to remember her by. But this ineloquent avatar of hers that lacked all her usual spunk didn't seem to be up to the task.

"Are you going to miss me?" asked James. But the twinkle in his eye which would have usually accompanied this sort of question was missing. He said it sadly.

"I certainly will miss setting eyes on your handsome visage," said Radha, determined to make one last attempt to salvage the situation. She could not let him leave when they were not themselves. She would not have him remember her like this.

James laughed. "You are going to give me a bloated head."

"Then I take that back. It won't do at all for your handsome head to be marred by bloating."

They both laughed at that and, for a moment, it seemed they had forgotten the past hour or so.

James looked into Radha's eyes and said, "You've got a very good visage yourself."

For a moment, Radha forgot to breathe. Through all this time, never once had he looked at her as he was looking at her now. His compliments had always been teasing. Radha had learned to handle those. She was completely taken aback by the deep tone of his voice and his piercing gaze. Surely, he could hear her heart hammering in her chest? She made a valiant attempt to regain her composure and said, in what she hoped was a teasing voice, "The impending journey has gotten to you. Or the light here is extremely flattering."

"Is it really so difficult to say a simple 'thank you'? I meant it, you know." And he took a stray lock of her hair between his fingers and tucked it behind her ear. As he withdrew his hand, his knuckles briefly brushed against her jaw. Radha now really could not breathe and they both stared at each other.

Finally, James looked away and said, "I should be going, I guess."

Radha said, "Bon voyage," and held out her hand. But James took her hand and drew her into a warm embrace saying, "We are past handshakes now. Thank you for everything."

He turned around and walked away with quick steps leaving Radha feeling inexplicably empty as she turned around herself and went to find the driver.

*

It had been three months since James had returned home. Life had gotten back into the routine that he was used to— working, swimming, meeting friends. His parents lived in the country in a sprawling house that had been in their family for ages. Courtesy of an ancestor who fought with the king centuries ago. James had no siblings, so after his parents, this would be his. He did love the house with its long corridors opening out onto balconies and the draughty nooks that he had hidden in when he was younger to escape punishment. This was where his dog lived as well, not with him in the city as he lived alone and travelled often on work. He did love coming home, to his dog. And, he was quite attached to his mother even if he didn't see her as often as she would have liked. Theirs was a relationship where neither spoke much, nor uttered obvious endearments, but which was strong. His relationship with his father was a lot more strained. They had always been formal with one another and James felt a certain lack of affection on his father's part for him. A disapproval of all the things he was, and James not being the most forgiving person, had let that drive a wedge in their relationship. And so, father and son had remained distant, with James' mother trying, unsuccessfully, to bring them closer.

There was a lot to manage in the estate but he left it to his father. He would eventually have to do it himself, but he put it off. James needed to be on his own. While he loved home, he would feel stifled if he stayed there under the disapproving and baleful eye of his father. Besides, he liked to work in the field he was in. He was an expert at it and loved it, so he could never drag himself away from that. He stayed in the city, but when he wanted to escape from it all, the madness of work, the bustle of city life, the expectations of his friends, and even the falsehood of some associates, he returned home.

That's why, as someone who never got really attached to anyone at all, he was surprised at his deep affection for Radha. She had pierced the shield around his cold heart and made him smile. James still remembered the night he left Bangalore. As he had gotten through the long lines of emigration and security, his thoughts had been with Radha. His head was filled with her soft perfume which he was convinced he could have recognized anywhere and would remember forever. The inflight entertainment had done little to distract him from his thoughts which kept returning to her face, visualizing its every contour, its every imperfection.

He avoided thinking of Radha or his days in India, but when he did, like today, he would go into an unexplained panic as he could not remember her face clearly or the smell of the perfume she wore. And for some reason, that depressed him more than anything else in the world. He would almost pick up his phone to check his photos to remind himself of how she looked but would always stop himself. He could never understand why he stopped himself. It was as if seeing her again would bring to the surface all the emotions he had managed to suppress these last few months. There really was no point in going down that road. Nothing could come of their attraction and it was best he never peeked into that Pandora's box again. But sometimes, a lady co-worker would be a bit too strident in an attempt to be heard, and he would think of Radha trying to make a mark for herself in a male-dominated corporate room. Occasionally, an odd argument would make him think of her annoying habit of always having to win an argument. And sometimes, a repartee from a colleague would remind him of the way Radha always had to have the last word. None of these qualities were very endearing but that's what James remembered of her the most. That's what still brought a wistful smile to his lips even after all these months. They had exchanged a few messages since he was back but they had always been perfunctory. Lacking the spark he had always enjoyed in their conversations. Perhaps this was because they were out of touch with the day-to-day happenings in each other's lives. Whatever the reason, their conversations were so different from what he was used to that he tended not to engage in any.

His cab came to a halt outside his workplace and brought him out of his reverie. He checked the time on his wristwatch. He was supposed to get on a video conference with Alex and his team in quarter of an hour. Alex had requested that James come on ten minutes earlier to go over the agenda and make sure they were all on the same page. James hurried to the VC room and logged in. Alex was already there and they greeted each other warmly. James had developed a lot of respect for Alex in the past few months even though they didn't often see eye to eye on many things as they were on opposite sides of the table. They had just started conversing, when James was surprised to see Radha rush in and then stop herself as she realized Alex was not alone.

"Sorry," stammered an embarrassed Radha. Then accusingly looked at Alex and said, "I thought your meeting didn't begin till a little later." As Alex explained to Radha that they had gotten together a little early, James allowed himself to stare at her. God, he had missed her. The slightly clumsy air, the flustered behaviour when caught unawares, the confused look on her face, the way she moved her index finger across the tip of her nose when she was embarrassed. It all came rushing back to him and then he noticed that Alex and Radha were watching him as he was staring at her. He must have missed what they said. Radha repeated, "I'm terribly sorry, James. I will leave you two alone. It was nice seeing you after so long." And just like that she was gone.

*

Later that evening, James decided to call her. Seeing her accidentally after so many months had made him realize that he really did want to continue being in touch with her. Moreover, he was expected to return to India soon and he might as well let her know. So what if nothing would come of it? So what if it would lead him down a torturous path of futility? So what if he risked scaring her away and ruining what they had? The last thing didn't matter anyway. They had nothing now. For a brief, wonderful time, it had seemed like they had everything and now there was just a void, a disappearing whisper of a day gone by, a ghost of a memory that was impossible to fully recollect, a fleeting touch of what they had shared which now slipped through his fingers as he tried to grasp it. Really there was nothing to lose, so he picked up his phone and dialled. He was just about to ring off when she picked up. He hated her unsure voice when she questioningly spoke his name.

"Yes, it's me. It was lovely seeing you today and I thought I'd call you. Is it too close to your bedtime?" And thinking of her in bed sent a weird but wonderful sensation coursing through him. Yup, he was still an adolescent idiot. How had he come to be this pathetic? He lit a cigarette to calm his nerves.

"How have you been? Why haven't you been in touch?"

"I could ask the same of you."

"But I asked first."

"Never mind. How's your dog?" James slapped his forehead at the stupid question. Her dog? Was that the best he could do?

"I didn't realize you took such a keen interest in my dog. But, since you asked, he is fine. I've also adopted a stray and Lucifer—that's my dog's name—is throwing a mighty sulk. The stray loves cheese and Lucifer probably thinks he is being cheated out of his inheritance. He brings the roof down when I feed him. The stray, of course, doesn't even bother barking back. Eats the cheese and walks off with all the dignity in the world making Lucifer look quite silly. But I'm rambling. This is what you get when you ask me about dogs."

"No, go on. I've kind of missed the rambling. I would hate for you to turn pauciloquent now."

"Please wait while I fetch a dictionary."

"I said that to get exactly this response. How's work?"

"Pretty decent. I got promoted."

"Congratulations! Now you no longer have to prove yourself."

"It's not like I was made the managing director. Of course, I still need to prove myself."

"Your poor colleagues. You will be riding roughshod over them, projecting the go-getter image."

"Huh?" Radha said after a long pause.

"I may be wrong, but at work you seemed a little aggressive. Taking on battles, getting your point across with a lot of force, sometimes even a little defensive. It's just that I saw you a bit outside the office when I was there and you were easy to be with. At work, you seemed a lot pricklier and a lot more focused on getting heard."

"You got all that from our short business association? I do appreciate the psychoanalysis."

Idiot! James cursed himself. She was obviously offended. And he who never judged people had done a character analysis when he was speaking to her after so long. "Sorry, that was poorly done of me. And I have managed to offend you like the very first time we met. I didn't mean it badly. It's as Sartre said: 'Hell is other people'. It's the image of you that people have and you fall prey to it and behave according to what people expect of you. It's a self-fulfilling cycle."

He could hear Radha chuckle self-consciously on the phone as she said, "Don't worry, I'm not offended. I was just taken aback a little. Did you ever study psychology? You are pretty good at this. Let me confess—I do put on a bit of an act at work. Sometimes, I've found it helps me to be taken seriously. Nothing against my co-workers, they are all great men. But at a sub-conscious level, I do believe it is difficult to be taken seriously as a woman. Maybe more so in the technology industry. Maybe you are right. Maybe I'm just prickly. But a part of me tells me I am right. That women in the corporate world do fight gender biases at a subliminal level. And to over-compensate, some of us have to seem a lot more vocal and aggressive. I have to say I'm impressed, though. You are quite perceptive."

"By the way, I'm back in India in a couple of weeks. We are wrapping up a milestone. It will be great to see you again, Radha, and relive the wonderful time we had."

"Uh-huh," came her answer. "Yes, see you soon. I'll check with Alex on when you are here."

"I'll tell you myself. Take care, Radha."

"You too, James."

"I can't wait to see you again." James rung off smiling to himself. He had embarrassed her, he was sure of it. She had a little routine when she was embarrassed, as he remembered.

She'd turn that slight shade of pink he had loved to see. She would self-consciously tuck her hair behind her ears. She would shuffle her feet the slightest bit. All actions that made her discomfiture very endearing. His heart filled with an unfamiliar warmth. Lord, he had missed her!

Chapter 14

There is no surer foundation for a beautiful friendship than a mutual taste in literature.

P G Wodehouse

___

The night James arrived in India he developed a horrible muscle pull in his back. As he lay writhing in pain in the hotel room, he considered his options. He would call the hotel reception and ask them to find a doctor. He had no idea how the medical system worked in India. Where would a non-citizen go? Were there designated hospitals? He really should have found out more. He was just about to ring the reception when it struck him to try Alex. As luck would have it, his number was unreachable. Curse his fortune. He was beginning to think he would pass out from the pain. He then decided to call Radha.   Even though it was past eight.

"Hello?" answered her voice. It seemed thick with sleep and despite his pain, he felt a stirring in his heart.

"Radha, this is James. Did I wake you? I'm extremely sorry."

"Oh no, I must have drifted off when I was reading. It's not too late at all," said Radha checking the time. "I've not even finished dinner. How are you? I was going to come see you tomorrow."

"Not too good, I'm afraid. I seem to have an unbearable pain in my back. I wasn't sure where I could show it and Alex's mobile seems switched off or unreachable."

"I'll be right there. I'll drive you to a hospital."

"Just like that?" asked James. "Will the hospital see me right away?"

Radha was confused at this. "What do you mean? Of course, they will."

"Oh? In the UK our NHS is different. We don't get seen immediately unless it's an emergency."

Radha assured him that there was no such system in place in India. One paid the consultation fees and saw the doctor. No matter who you were or from which country or what insurance you held. If you could make the payment at the registration desk, the doctor would see you. That's all there was to that. Promising him she would be there as soon as possible, Radha rung off.

Sometime later they were sitting opposite the doctor as he explained that the pull was temporary and that an injection would give James considerable relief. He would then have to ensure he didn't stress the muscle for another week or so. Radha seemed to know the doctor personally and in fact had called him from the car and requested him to stay back in the hospital till she arrived with James. James was very surprised he had complied and asked Radha about it later who explained to him that her grandmother had the unfortunate habit of tripping and falling ever so often as she scurried around the house.

Despite all warnings to be careful, her grandmother would take a tumble and would need to be rushed to the hospital. This doctor was her grandmother's favourite and she would always insist on seeing him. As a result, the doctor was quite familiar with Radha and her family. But as they sat in front of the doctor, James did not know this and so he found it strange when Radha thanked him too warmly for seeing James. He was surprised to see the young doctor reach across and pat Radha's palm equally warmly. But what was most surprising to James was the unreasonable fit of jealousy that came over him when the doctor took Radha's hand. Life had to be kidding him. All that putting distance between them seemed to have mattered not in the slightest. He was the same fool he had been when he had seen Radha last.

"I called Alex on his personal number," said Radha on the way back. "Apparently he had to take off at short notice due to an emergency regarding a friend. He is stuck there and will be unable to come into work till the day after. He was going to call you in the morning and let you know. Anyway, I have assured him that you will be in my safe hands tomorrow."

"That is indeed very reassuring. I cannot thank you enough, Radha."

"Please don't worry about it. It just struck me—why don't you join my family for dinner tomorrow? My uncle is visiting and you just might be entertained by my loony relatives. And it would be convenient to be around you, in case you suddenly need to be rushed off to the hospital."

"That will be fantastic, thank you. I would love to join you," said James ignoring the inexplicable soaring of his heart. "But why the smile?"

"Just thinking of how you might be able to survive my family tomorrow. You manage that and you prove you have nerves of steel."

"They can't be that bad!"

Radha only smiled at this and said, "Famous last words. I'll see you tomorrow at work."

*

The Embassy Golf Links Business Park is a sprawling campus, themed, as one would guess from the name, around golf. Boards describing celebrated golf courses dot the beautifully landscaped area around the office buildings. If someone drove to this office space from the nearby Ejipura, they would be struck by the stark differences between the two worlds. The Golf Park is the very epitome of affluence and privilege. The golf theme, the swanky glass buildings, the manicured lawns and the wide roads flanked by perfectly trimmed and neat shrubs, all scream of an entitled India very different from the aspiring India that is the majority of the country. But like every other dichotomy in India, these two worlds also co-exist in a symbiotic relationship—different, but inexorably bound together.

Adjoining the Embassy Golf Links Park is the golf course. The course is visible from some parts of the office campus and many an office-goer cast envious eyes at those playing golf during a working day as they trudge past to their offices. As James drove to Radha's office within the campus, he too espied the Golf Club where he and Radha had had lunch on his last trip. It seemed like ages ago, yet the memory was fresh in his head. They had discussed Radha's favourite authors, James remembered.

"It's a toss-up between Jane Austen, Daphne du Maurier and Somerset Maugham," Radha had said. "Austen for her ability to paint vivid colours into an ordinary country life. Her books are nothing like the page turners that are bestsellers nowadays where something is always happening and we careen from one twist to the other. It's plain and simple beautiful writing about ordinary lives. And the romance! Without any explicit words or actions at all! Mr Darcy has to be my all-time favourite hero. He makes my heart pound every time I read Pride and Prejudice and I must have read it a dozen times at the very least."

James had looked amused and quizzed Radha on why Daphne du Maurier had made the cut. Radha's eyes had lit up. "I'm not eloquent enough to describe her books. The foreboding, the anticipation, the romance. She is a master story-teller. She makes me want to be timid wife, an intrepid, adventurous woman, a scheming cousin all at once!"

James remembered having guessed Rebecca, Frenchman's Creek, My Cousin Rachel much to Radha's surprise who was surprised that a man read Daphne du Maurier. She had always believed her to be a woman's author, Radha had told James. She had also told him that thanks to du Maurier, Cornwall was on Radha's number one place to visit and she was waiting for the day when she could see the angry waves crash against the rocks of Cornwall as described by the author. James remembered offering to return Radha's hospitality and show her around Cornwall. Well, it would not do to reminisce of days gone by, James thought wistfully as he came back to the present and climbed the stairs to his workspace.

*

Radha was chatting with Lakshmi on her way to work. She

had gotten slightly late as Paati had insisted on oiling her hair in the morning. When Radha had protested, Paati had brooked no dissent insisting that modern habits of using a conditioner in lieu of the age-old tradition of massaging the hair with oil had turned Radha's hair a dull and dry brown. There was never any arguing with Paati so Radha had suffered the routine while her grandmother doused her hair with oil steeped in neem leaves and hibiscus flowers and reminded Radha how grateful she should be to get this homemade oil when there were enough companies bottling the same ingredients at exorbitant prices.

She told Lakshmi about the hospital dash last evening.

"So, now you are Florence Nightingale?" said Lakshmi, voice dripping with sarcasm.

"Don't be silly. I didn't nurse him back to health, merely drove him to a doctor."

"Don't be so literal, Radha. I was playing the wit. I have to wander from the truth. What is with the two of you anyway? With this now-on, now-off thing? You didn't breathe a word about him for the past few months and now you are again full of stories of him. Don't explain; you'll just say some half-assed thing and annoy me more. Do what you want, it's your funeral. But don't say I didn't warn you if your heart is broken. By the way, you remember I'm off on my two-week holiday from the day after? Be good. I won't be around to save you."

"Have a great trip. Lucky you! Seeing Venice. Now you can die."

"Huh?"

"It's a saying. *See Venice and die,* meaning there is nothing else to live for after one sees Venice."

"You don't have to explain the saying. I was unaware of it but I'm not dumb; I can understand the meaning of a simple sentence. God knows where you read all these sayings. Get a life!"

"I will. In the meantime, you enjoy yours. Bye. Have a wonderful time!"

"Bye. I'll send you a postcard."

*

Radha met James over lunch. He groaned at the end of it complaining that all this eating couldn't be good.

"I have to disagree. A delightful meal can be nothing but good. It feeds the soul. You have to balance the sheer happiness against any possible drawback of being unfit. It's quite like a balance sheet."

James laughed and said, "My chartered accountant cousin would approve of the analogy."

"Your cousin is a chartered accountant? That's impressive!" said Radha, her eyes widening with awe. "I took accountancy in my management degree and I have the dubious distinction of never, ever having balanced one sheet. Your cousin has my undying respect."

James laughed. "I'll make sure I tell him. So, what have you been up to these past few months?"

"Nothing too fancy, I'm afraid. Just played out the humdrum routine that is the essence of my ordinary life."

"Don't underestimate the value of an ordinary existence. Excitement is highly overrated!"

"Oh! I completely agree," concurred Radha. "But it doesn't make for a nice story when someone asks you what you did. How spectacularly our tomb raider Lara Croft would answer that question!"

They both laughed and Radha suggested that James should visit Kerala during this trip.

"I've heard of Kerala. I would love to see the backwaters on a houseboat. I'm told it is fabulous."

"I'll probably be killed for saying this but that houseboat routine is highly overrated. The houseboats usually have a musty smell and then when the engine is running, there is the ever-present industrial smell of burning fuel. Of course, the backwaters are absolutely lovely and a treat to watch. What with the trees on the banks almost stooping low to kiss their own reflections in the water."

James smiled. "I had no idea a poet lurked within your heart."

"That was a bit over the top, wasn't it?"

"No, I loved the way you put it. So, I get it—Kerala is an absolute yes. The magnificence of the houseboat experience is to be taken with a pinch of salt. What else must I visit?"

"How on earth did our conversation veer towards tourism?" pondered Radha aloud.

"Your guess is as good as mine," said James and there was the lopsided smile Radha loved.

Before Radha could stop herself, she blurted, "You have a terrific smile."

James stopped short and looked at her in surprise. What might have been five seconds seemed like an eternity to Radha as she wondered if it was ever possible to reverse the direction of those words right back into her mouth and direct them to stay in her mind, where they should have stayed to begin with. But James did respond, his endearing smile broadening. "I do believe you rendered me temporarily speechless."

Radha scrambled to gather her wits and replied, "And is you being speechless an uncommon occurrence?"

"Not really. But it was a pleasant occurrence. You won't hear me complain if you want to render me speechless again."

"Don't count on it," responded Radha sulkily.

"Might I return the compliment? You have a beautiful smile too."

"Really? Couldn't you at least think of something original?"

"I couldn't think. You were directing said smile at me."

"Don't be silly."

"And yet you've turned that charming shade of pink," teased James.

"Whatever!" said Radha, racing to change the subject. "Did you like the rasam? Or what you folks call the mulligatawny soup?"

"In all my life, I never used the word 'mulligatawny'."

"Did you know the origin of the word 'mulligatawny' is actually Tamil? It literally means pepper-water in the unanglicized, correct form."

"Each moment with you is a revelation."

"Go ahead. Be cheeky. See if I care," returned Radha with a scowl.

James reached across the table and patted Radha's hand. "Sorry."

"Your smile tells me you are not in the least bit sorry."

"I feel like smiling around you," said James solemnly. "It has nothing to do with how apologetic I am or am not feeling. The smile comes unbidden. Cross my heart and hope to die."

Radha laughed. "It's hard to be annoyed with you when you use the expressions of a seven-year-old." James shrugged and Radha continued, "But as one of our leading stars said in a Bollywood movie— *bade bade deshon main aisi choti choti baatein hoti rehti hain.* So, you are quite forgiven."

"I have no idea what that means, but who is this much-quoted actor?"

"His name is Shah Rukh Khan. Even Barack Obama quoted this dialogue when he was in India. Played to the gallery, did Obama, and we Indians unfailingly fell for it. Anyway, Shah Rukh Khan is the quintessential romantic hero. In every movie he does this hold-his-arms-out routine and it has become his signature move. Lots of women go crazy when he does that. I have to admit that every time I am in the Mumbai airport, I hope he is there too and spots me and offers me a role in his next movie. I so do want to be the heroine he holds his arms out for."

James laughed and said, "Lucky man." Then, without giving Radha a chance to react, he asked her for directions to her house. Radha offered to take him but he had some work he wanted finished off and said he would meet her directly at her home.

CHAPTER 15

Sell crazy someplace else; we're all stocked up here.

Jack Nicholson, As Good As It Gets

Later in the evening, Revati Iyer was whizzing around the house like a whirlwind. Moving bric-a-bracs infinitesimally, plumping cushions, rearranging the perfectly arranged orchids and, of course, yelling at the harassed cook, Usha, every two minutes.

Radha and her maternal grandmother looked at her with an indulgent yet exasperated air.

"Please slow down, Amma," begged Radha as she sipped her after-work-perk-me-up tea. "I'm getting a headrush whipping my head around as I attempt to keep track of your movements!" And then turned to her grandmother and said, "Why can't you control your daughter, Paati?"

Paati answered in a voice that was surprisingly strong for an eighty-year-old. "It's all your grandfather's fault. He spoilt her silly dancing to her every tune. And your father never tried to check her as well. It's now impossible to change her. She will do precisely what she wants. No one listens to me anyway."

Radha rolled her eyes. Her Paati always got exactly what she wanted while all along playing the ever-suffering victim card. Her mother had her grandmother's genes. The apple certainly never fell far from the tree. But Radha loved her paati. She had been with them since Radha was a little girl and had been her closest ally growing up as a single child. Paati had shielded Radha from her parents when she got in trouble, gotten her to love History by studying it with her, let her sleep with her when she watched a scary movie and was too scared to sleep alone and slipped her tuck money on many a school day so that Radha could eat corn on cob with her friends after school. Radha and her Paati were thick as thieves.

But most of all, Paati was Radha's in-house doctor. From stomach-ache to a burning eye to dandruff to bad hair days, her grandmother had an unpronounceable herb for every ailment. She would boil weird herbs and spices, stirring them over a kitchen pot and Radha would watch in awe. "You look like a witch, Paati," she would say. "But a good, lovable witch."

Radha was brought back to the present by her granduncle's voice. He had arrived just this morning for a short stay and, as usual, was driving everyone mad. He was a brilliant man, having always finished any school and university level with kids at least two years older. Of course, those were the days it was allowed. Nowadays, no one could study in a class unless he or she had reached the correct age for the said class. He had joined the Merchant Navy and long years as an engineer on ship had made him almost deaf. He did have hearing aids, but they had such an acoustic mixture of feedback and static that Hari walked around sounding like R2D2 from Star Wars. So, everyone discouraged him from wearing it. As a result, one had to shout out everything for him. At times, Radha was convinced he heard some of his family's cheeky comments quite clearly but used his hearing problems as an excuse to completely ignore them.

"Have you created a Facebook account for me, Radha?" asked Hari. "I told you the moment I landed, and if I miss the El Clásico match tonight, it will all be your fault."

Revati sighed wearily and paused from plumping the cushions for the fourth time. "Firstly, why would a football match that is played more than once a year be called El Clásico? You'd imagine that if it was so classic, it would be less frequent. Secondly, you are Indian and neither affiliated to Real Madrid nor Barcelona. Why can't you just watch cricket like the rest of us? And thirdly, what sort of idiocy is this? Telecasting a match only on Facebook TV?"

Of course, Hari did not find it necessary to answer any question and ignored his niece. He walked off with a, "Make sure it is done before your guest arrives, Radha."

She knew it was far easier just arranging for him to watch the match and got to her feet to get it done. Otherwise, her granduncle would just nag her till kingdom come.

"Radha, please change when you are done!" shouted Revati behind her. "I hope you weren't planning to entertain your office guest in the clothes you are wearing."

"It's really above and beyond the call of duty that I'm inviting him anyway." But Radha was just baiting her mother. She intended getting dressed up anyway. She wanted to look pretty when James visited.

"Nevertheless, you have called him and dress you shall. And for heaven's sake, choose something bright. Not the usual dull shades of brown and grey that forms the majority of your wardrobe," replied Revati in her usual manner of not brooking any further discussion and bustled off to bully the cook.

Paati said with a chuckle, "It's a real wonder one of the staff has not slipped some poison into your mother's food till now." They both knew that Revati was a good employer and below the bustling exterior and abrasive manner lurked a kind-hearted woman and that's why the staff put up with her nagging. But grandmother and granddaughter tittered conspiratorially anyway before Radha walked off to get the blasted FB TV in order.

*

An hour later, the doorbell went off and Lucifer started with his welcome routine. Though the jury was still out on whether visitors to the household would concur that annoyed barks and menacing growls constituted a welcome.

It was James, and Radha tried to still the mad beating of her heart when she saw him. Lucifer threw himself on James and when Radha struggled to control him, he said, "Please don't bother. I love dogs and they usually love me. I'm sure he won't harm me."

Radha groaned mentally. Drop dead gorgeous *and* loves dogs? This was killing her! Of course, Radha knew Lucifer was all bark and no bite but she rarely told any visitors that. It gave her a perverse pleasure to have them be scared of entering the house. But Lucifer seemed to be licking James' hands as though it was a cheese cube, his favourite food. And, in these circumstances, Radha could hardly pretend that Lucifer was a vicious guard dog. So, she stepped aside and said, "Come right in, please. But you will have his hair all over your clothes. Don't say I didn't warn you."

Radha introduced James to everyone after he was settled in. Of course, Revati charmed the socks off him. She was always like that. Could make friends easily and talk nineteen to the dozen and put anyone at ease. Hari was his usual mad self. Made some comments about Manchester United and never bothered to even pretend he heard James' response. Radha gave a it's-not-your-fault-and-don't-take-it-personally shrug and James looked comforted by that. And then Paati hobbled in and James did an awkward namaste.

She smiled at him and spoke in English that would make the Queen proud. "How do you do? We have been eagerly expecting you and now we can start off the party in right earnest."

James looked dumbstruck at her.

Radha said, "For your own sake, please do not express surprise at her English. She was speaking fluent English before you learnt how to say *mama*. She's an Economics major and remember I told you about one of my relatives suing an Englishwoman for defamation? That was Paati's father."

Paati replied, "That's a story for another day. Suffice to say, she spoke without complete knowledge on Hinduism and my father took her to the cleaners. Now you have to try my potato fry starter. It's my signature dish and a special favourite of Radha's."

"That's hardly a reason for him to eat it, Paati," scolded Radha. Then she turned to Lucifer and said, "Will you please stop begging and embarrassing me, Luke? And you've drooled all over the place!"

"Looks like the irrigation problems of rural India could be solved by Lucifer," said James, looking indulgently at Lucifer.

"I am beyond ashamed," said Radha. "Now you'll imagine I have been a horrible failure in training my dog."

"Don't worry. My fellow is equally badly behaved."

"Really?" asked an incredulous Radha. "Because my friend who stays in England told me that dogs were very quiet there. She specifically mentioned that dogs were better behaved than our dogs in India. They hardly bark, if I am to believe her. Just sit at people's feet like dolls."

"Lucifer loves my mixture of yoghurt and rice too. He's rather accustomed to our diet," said Paati proudly as though no one had spoken in the interim.

"Really, Paati. This is hardly something to brag about," said Radha. "No self-respecting dog likes yoghurt."

James just laughed at that and picked up a piece of the potato fry. It looked rather an angry red for his taste but he did not want to offend Radha's grandmother. He swallowed the piece only to be confronted by Paati's hopeful and eager eyes. "It's very delicious, ma'am," he said, feeling a little untruthful, as it was rather too spicy for his taste.

"You must call me Paati. That's Tamil for grandmother. Everyone does."

"That's only because you are as old as Methusaleh," Radha teased her.

At the dining table, Radha tried to educate James on the fare. "This is pumpkin in a coconut gravy. You do know pumpkin?"

"Yes, although we usually just eviscerate them once a year during Halloween. I've never eaten them much before."

"Eviscerate? I shall never really look at pumpkins the same way again," said Radha with a mock shudder. "I should warn you that not many people even in the North of India will eat this pumpkin-coconut concoction."

"Nonsense!" scolded Revati. "Will you let him taste it and decide for himself. Don't pay her any heed Mr Rutherford, she's just teasing you. She loves it herself but has been giving me a hard time since the evening saying I should have cooked Indian food that you are familiar with. Which is really more North Indian cuisine since that is what is more easily available in England. Tikka and the ilk, you know. But I thought you should taste something different. Here, pair that with the stringy rice noodles we have here. I'm sure you will love it."

"Now he can't even say otherwise, Amma. Not when you have already decided for him that he will love it."

"Don't sass me, Radha," said Revati with a finality that meant the conversation was at end.

James rose from the table quite satiated. "This was the mildest yet most flavourful Indian meal I have ever had, ma'am. Thank you very much for introducing me to a cuisine I am completely unused to," he said to Revati.

Revati beamed and bustled them over to the living room for coffee. Paati handed James a package wrapped in newspaper.

"I don't like to gift wrap and add to the mounds of rubbish we accumulate every day. I hope you don't mind," said Paati.

"Not in the least," said James graciously as he put away the package.

"Oh! Do open it!" urged Paati. "I want to see if you like it."

Radha rolled her eyes. It was not as if James would say he didn't like it, even if he didn't, she thought. Her family was really dense. But James seemed to be really spellbound by the beautiful Ganesha her grandmother had bought him. Paati used her age to escape stepping out of the house but when it came to shopping, she would be ready with an alacrity that belied her age. Her partner in crime was Madan, who would drive her to the ends of the earth if she wished it. He would hold her hand and lead her carefully up the steps of her favourite saree or handicraft store. The latter was a store called Chandni, The Divine Gallery on MG Road. Paati was especially partial to the owner of the store so she bought all her idols only from there.

"It's a lovely Ganesha, thank you, Paati," said James.

Radha stared at him.

"What?" he asked under his breath.

"I'm just marvelling you didn't call him Elephant God like most foreigners do. And loving you ever so slightly for it."

"Hold that last thought," said James with a devastating smile and turned back to Paati to continue discussing the Ganesha idol. As expected, Paati launched into high praise for Sultan, the owner of the store in question.

"Such a well-mannered man, so knowledgeable, so soft-spoken," she continued and one would have imagined Sultan was her only son and heir and not merely the owner of a store she frequented.

After what seemed like an eternity, Paati finally ran out of wonderful adjectives to describe Sultan and finished with, "You must visit that store, Mr Rutherford. You will find fine gifts to take home."

"I most certainly will," replied James, touching Paati's arm. "But, please, you must call me James."

Paati smiled in acknowledgement, bid goodnight citing her advancing years and retired to her room. Soon Revati and Radha's granduncle, Hari, also decided to call it a day and Radha offered to play some music.

"Dire Straits?"

James looked at her in amazement. "Did you know that is among my favourite bands?"

"I didn't. I just happen to love them too," replied Radha as the strains of Sultans of Swing started in the background. "You know you were pretty lucky to be spared a massive argument over dinner. We can fight on just about anything, can our family. And, usually, having company is rarely a deterrent. But somehow, today we were all on our best behaviour."

"Then I must consider myself unlucky," replied James. "I would have been happy to witness a good argument."

"Of course! Who doesn't like some free entertainment?" said Radha mockingly.

"No, it's not that," said James earnestly. "You seemed to share a very easy vibe with your family. You even call your granduncle by his name. My family is a lot more formal. So that was refreshing to see."

"And it would have been even more refreshing to see us trying to gouge each other's eyes out," chuckled Radha.

"Most undoubtedly." Romeo and Juliet started to play and James said, "Want to dance?"

Radha was a little taken aback and nodded feebly, "Sure."

The next fifteen minutes were a daze for Radha. She could not remember when she had had a more romantic quarter of an hour. Neither could she remember, at the end of those fifteen minutes, when she had gone from dancing at an arm's length with James, to being enfolded in a warm embrace, James' chin resting on the top of her head. This was madness, panicked Radha as the music stopped and she stumbled away clumsily.

"I should probably be headed back," said James, himself looking a bit dazed.

"Sure. Can I drop you back?"

"No, thank you. It is quite late and I should be able to get myself a cab. I couldn't possibly drag you out this late in the night," said James, simultaneously whipping out his phone to book a cab.

An unbidden thought came rushing to Radha's mind that she would happily be dragged anywhere by him at any time of the day and night. Luckily, she had not said that aloud and chuckled to herself.

James looked up from his phone and asked, "What's the joke?"

"Never mind. My mind wandered," replied Radha sheepishly. "Would you like a spot of tea while we wait? And please do notice how I said 'spot of tea' exactly like you Brits do."

James laughed and exaggerating his already British accent said, "I rather think I'd like that very much."

*

As James returned to his hotel, he let his thoughts remain on Radha. James realized that he'd had a really wonderful evening. Radha's family had been quite delightful and he had felt very much at home. Though she had warned him that the family had a streak of madness, he had liked them. Quirky and whimsical and unreasonable, maybe. Crazy, too. But he had liked them. At times, he had envied Radha the easy relationship she shared with her family. Certainly, it was uncommon for someone to have that. He hoped she realized that. He really had nothing like that with anyone.

He was not going to dwell on what devil had possessed him when he had blurted his request to her to dance. But he would dance with her a hundred more times if he could, of that he was sure.

He pulled out his mobile and texted Radha before he could change his mind.

Thanks for dinner.

I was thinking, do you want to go out with me tomorrow night?

Two blue ticks. She had read his message. He signed out quickly, almost too afraid to see her answer. Well, it was done.

He had asked this maddening Indian girl, with a clear genetic streak of craziness, out on a date. God help him.

CHAPTER 16

If music be the food of love, play on.

William Shakespeare

Radha felt light-headed the next evening as she criss-crossed her room, ransacking her cupboards and drawers for something to wear. Usually, she wasn't too particular about how she looked, but if any situation called for vanity to come to the fore, this was it. Never before had her wardrobe seemed so inadequate to her. Maybe she should have just refused James last night. He was anyway a coward for asking her out on WhatsApp. It would have served him right if she had. But her traitorous heart had wrested control from her brain and forced her fingers to type out an acceptance. More fool her.

It was a small mercy that Lakshmi was travelling. Otherwise, she would have been here now, like a maestro in an opera, orchestrating the whole afternoon and evening, telling her what to wear, doing up her hair, choosing accessories, being Radha's guide on the course 'How to be a Coquette 101' and generally making Radha miserable in the process.

James had said he would pick her up but Radha didn't want

it to become too big a deal so she had suggested they meet at the restaurant directly. She had given him the directions to the 13th Floor, Ebony. At the top of one of the retail buildings in the heart of Bangalore city, Ebony offers an almost unmatched view of the central part of Bangalore. With Bangalore's weather being what it is, sitting outside in the open-air section and looking down on the city lights below while floating magically above the mayhem creates a lovely dining experience.

Radha had asked James to wait downstairs if he arrived early and he was. He had not spotted her so she took the opportunity to look at him and take in his Greek God looks. Surely, he belonged on the big screen. He was so nice to talk with and they seemed to have such a complete wavelength match mentally that Radha had almost forgotten how handsome James was. Looking at him from afar without his wit and humour distracting her, she realized anew that her James was quite the dish to be eaten. She waved to him and his answering warm smile caused her heart to skip a beat. She walked up to him and squinted up into his face.

"Hello!" she said lamely.

"And hello right back."

She laughed and pointed to the entrance and said, "Shall we?" and got his overly polite answer of "Right behind you."

As they waited for the elevator to empty out, someone rushed out of it and Radha stepped backwards without thinking and bumped right into James who was quite literally, it seemed, right behind her.

"Terribly sorry," said Radha as he steadied her.

"You won't hear me complain. I'm not in the least bit sorry," whispered James into her ear.

He watched her turn his favourite shade of beetroot and steadied his own senses. *Did someone have the right to smell quite so wonderful,* he thought to himself. Perhaps he should ask her what perfume she used. It was quite delightful. Though what he would do with the name he didn't know. It's not that he could buy a bottle and sniff it occasionally. It was Radha that lent the perfume its characteristic bouquet.

To Radha's relief, James loved the place and they chatted about this and that over dinner. So far, this 'date' had gone no differently from any of the meals they had shared. James did mention again how glad he was to have been invited over to her place the previous day. He also told her that he found Radha's family quite charming.

"That's only because we were the best versions of ourselves yesterday," laughed Radha. "You were so lucky that you weren't even forced to have yoghurt. My family finds it very odd if anyone refuses yoghurt. You got off easy."

When they finished dinner and were waiting for the bill, Radha urged James to try the 'saunf'. "You must try these sweetened fennel seeds. They really do help in digesting one's food. Besides, it freshens the breath too and leaves a nice aftertaste."

"And what would I do with fresh breath at this point?"

"That is surely a matter for you alone to decide on, sir," said Radha impishly, not taking the bait.

"You are doing that again, Radha. Running away."

"She who runs away lives to fight another day," came her prompt response and she suggested they walk off the food by taking an auto rickshaw to the nearby legal and executive centre of the city and taking a stroll there. James teased her about being a sucker for punishment by again putting herself at the mercy of her bete noire, an auto driver. But he looked quite impressed by the Vidhan Soudha, the seat of Karnataka's state legislature and the imposing Attara Kacheri opposite from it when he reached there. The Attara Kacheri is a red brick sprawling building that houses the High Court of Karnataka in Bangalore. The tall columns and the numerous corridors and hallways with their balustrades somehow reflect the majesty of the law. In the mornings, if one is outside, one can see lawyers in flowing black robes walk busily, weaving their way through the court halls, moving splashes of black amid the red and green background created by the brick building and trees.

As they strolled down the broad pavement outside the wall of the court, their fingers brushed and James took Radha's hand. She didn't pull it away but closed her fingers around his. They passed a policeman who stared at them.

"Why is that policeman staring at us?" asked James.

"Because we Indians never think that staring is rude. Even if you catch someone staring at you, they will never look away in embarrassment but continue to stare as if it is their God-given right. And anyway, I'm holding hands with a foreigner. That's enough to interest him. He must be seeing a lot of Romeo-Juliets around here, but your white skin is certainly a novelty."

"Is that what we are? Romeo and Juliet?" asked James softly.

"I should certainly hope not! Highly over-rated, their love. It's easy to be infatuated with someone and then go out in a blaze of glory very quickly after. A true test of love is one that stands the cruelty of time. Getting past the initial buzz, accepting the other's foibles, compromising with things that cannot be resolved, finding happiness in the little moments of togetherness. Adding up the small moments of joy till the sum is enough to make the marriage work. And, growing old together without one killing the other even if the motive and opportunity presents itself."

"There you go again. Completely side-lining my question. You must have the last word, mustn't you, even if it is completely unrelated to the topic of discussion?" asked James.

"Damned if I do, damned if I don't," pouted Radha. "If I don't engage, I'm running away; if I do, I'm trying to have the last word."

"There's no winning with you, is there?"

Radha winked at James at this and said, "The occasional person might win. But I do make it very difficult." They walked on and James heard Radha humming a tune.

"What are you singing?"

Radha said apologetically, "Sorry, I don't even realize I am humming at times. It's one of my favourite songs. It's by India's very own musical genius AR Rahman. It goes *rehna tu, hain jaise tu, thoda sa dard tu, thoda sakoon*. Loosely translates to 'continue being the person you are, the cause of a little bit of my pain but the source of my contentment; sometimes a gentle zephyr, at others a storm; sometimes smooth as silk but at other times coarse; I never want you to change; you are just right—neither too much nor too little'. It's really very poetic."

"Every bit of that sounded like you," whispered James as he pulled her into his arms, looked deep into her eyes and bent his lips to hers in the lightest of kisses. Radha staggered back and looked up into James' eyes which looked strangely glazed.

"You know we don't do that in India in public," she finally said after they had looked into each other's eyes for what appeared to be an eternity.

"I should be sorry but I'm not. I couldn't help myself," said James and gently stroked her lips with his thumb. "The only way to get rid of temptation is to yield to it. Resist it, and your soul grows sick with longing for the things it has forbidden to itself."

"The picture of Dorian Gray? Did we read and love the same books? Though I prefer the other quote by Oscar Wilde: 'I can resist anything except temptation'. Much briefer! Anyway, shouldn't we be going back?"

"Must we?" came James' wistful response.

Radha thought to herself that this was just the kind of comment that did not help her resolve but didn't voice her thoughts. Instead, she said, "All good things must come to an end."

"About that. Who came up with that silly rule?" James answered with a wry smile but tucked her arm in his arm and started walking back.

Chapter 17

When I look into your eyes
I can see a love restrained
But darlin' when I hold you
Don't you know I feel the same
Nothin' lasts forever
And we both know hearts can change
And it's hard to hold a candle
In the cold November rain

Guns N' Roses

James felt he had known Radha forever. It was as simple as that. He could not pinpoint when a mild attraction had metamorphized into what he felt for Radha now. In a short span, she had become his dearest friend. But she was so much more. He enjoyed her company immensely, so much so that he missed her terribly when she wasn't around. He didn't speak much when they were together but it brought him great joy just to listen to her prattle on. She was reserved with everyone else, and he loved that he was special enough for her to be chatty only with him. He loved to watch her animated face as she made a catty remark about someone or bemoaned the behaviour of another or lamented about the state of the world. It was getting increasingly tough to stop himself from gathering her in his arms and kissing her senseless. He couldn't think of a better way of quietening her. And, at times, when she sat before him, so close yet so far away, he could actually feel his heart explode with pain. Those crappy romance novels actually got that right. He now knew for sure that the sudden searing pain through his heart was a reality for someone in love.

Once he had had the insane urge to tilt her head, bend his face and bite her neck. She had caught him staring and asked what he was thinking of and he answered, "Count Dracula". It took a moment for the import of his words to register with her and, when it did, he loved the pink that mushroomed on her cheek. He loved that she immediately understood what he was thinking. He loved that he could make her blush so easily. He loved how she looked at him from underneath her lashes when he rubbed his knuckles along her chin. He loved the provocative upward tilt of her chin as she dared him to come good on his unspoken promises. He loved that he felt like a callow youth around her. He loved her. With a certainty he had never felt before.

He was so glad that Radha was joining them for dinner that evening. The team had had an offsite at a lovely heritage hotel the past two days and he had missed seeing her. But Alex had asked her to drive up to the hotel the last night and join them for dinner. James hadn't spoken to her much through dinner but now he, Alex and Radha were nursing their last drink, well after everyone else had retired.

Alex stifled a yawn and got up. "I think I'll call it a day. Are you going to get back okay, Radha?"

"I'll be fine. I'm leaving soon anyway. Don't worry and get to bed. You look dead on your feet."

"He looks most reluctant to leave you with me," said James as they watched Alex's retreating figure. "Perhaps he worries about your virtue?"

Radha laughed at this and rubbed her arms. It was getting cold. James took his jacket off and wrapped it around her. Radha closed her eyes as she took in the warmth of the jacket. It smelt of him, and the faint smell of cigarettes. Any other time, that would be a put off, but not with James.

"What?" asked James as Radha realized she had zoned out. Could anyone be more lovestruck? She was behaving like those heroines on Netflix.

"Nothing. You reminded me of Sir Walter Raleigh."

"Except there's no puddle of water and you are no queen."

"Hey!!"

"I'd pick you over Elizabeth any day."

"I'm flattered, I guess. Since she's cold in her grave for four hundred years."

He bent down and kissed her cheek. "I missed you."

"I missed you more." She replied with that shy smile that had begun to drive him nuts.

"Of course, you have to do everything better," James teased her but the indulgent smile he gave her made Radha's heart do a little flip.

Radha interlaced her fingers with James and hung on to his arm with her other hand. She leaned her head on his shoulder. What was her mom always telling her? Carpe diem. Seize the day. She had had enough of this pussy-footing around her relationship with James. She was just going to tell him how she really felt about him. Not the teasing camaraderie but the deep love she felt. She had always been reluctant to bare her soul to him but these few days away had got her thinking that she didn't want him to be unaware of her real feelings for him. Of course, there were a thousand reasons this would not work, being in different continents being the least of them, but there was the one all-important reason she just had to try. She loved him. It was as simple as that. And she had to tell him that. She guessed the norm was that the man always made the first move but this was the twenty-first century for crying out loud. She hated that even today mainstream entertainment perpetuated the bias that it was up to the guy to declare his love. Sometimes go down on a knee. When would the world get over these clichés? She wasn't anyway planning to go down on a knee. It wasn't marriage she was considering. Just laying her heart before him and hoping he wouldn't trample all over it.

So tell him she did.

James sat looking at her without saying a word as she poured her heart out. And then said, "Do you want to come up to my room, Radha?"

He was looking at her so intently, Radha couldn't breathe. "I think I'll head back. It's quite late."

"Of course."

*

James shut his hotel door, slumped against it and whacked his forehead. Could he have messed up anymore? She had taken a leap of faith and he had just sat there. Unable to believe what he was hearing. She had always been so glib with him, and he with her. For his part, he had always been afraid of scaring her away with the intensity of his feelings so he hid them under a cloak of frivolity. And she had just taken his breath away. As he had sat and listened to her—earnest voice, bright eyes—he had never loved her more. And hence the silly request to come to his room.

If anyone needed a cold shower now, it was him. It was freezing but it would serve him right and, more importantly, cool his ardour. The doorbell rang and he opened it, mentally cursing, and with the most unfriendly look he could muster.

It was Radha.

The two of them looked at each other for what seemed an eternity and then James pulled her in, shut the door, cradled her face in his hands and then kissed her like a man possessed.

*

Later, they ordered in some tea. Apparently just about anything put Radha in the mood for tea, James thought with a smile, but held his peace.

"Why the thoughtful look?" he murmured against her lips.

"Wishing I had sexier lingerie," pouted Radha.

James laughed. "You are perfect. Even in a sack." And ducked as Radha flung a pillow at him. "And definitely perfect in THE sack too," said James with a wink.

Radha made a face at him. "I'd better head out before anyone sees me. I have anyway crashed your team building exercise."

James kissed the corner of her mouth and looked deeply into her eyes. "I've had a mind-blowing night."

Radha's breath caught and she desperately changed the subject. She just didn't know how to react to his intensity. "I'm going to Mumbai tomorrow. Shall I meet you for coffee the day after when I'm back? I'll text you the location and time."

"Coffee? Seriously? When all I would be thinking about is ripping your clothes off?"

"Eww. Don't use corny soap opera dialogues on me."

"Way to cut a man down to size, Radha!" laughed James as she let herself out.

*

The water in the lake appeared a bluish-green and the fog over the lake seemed to merge with it where the water kissed the horizon. A brightly coloured butterfly flitted between the various hydrangea bushes, now alighting on a blue one, now on a purple one, as though it was spoiled for choice and couldn't make up its mind which nectar it preferred. Somewhere in the distance, a church bell pealed and the fragrance of incense sticks wafted over the air. The haze impeded James' vision but without seeing anything, he was sure the figure that approached him was Radha. He could feel her presence even before she appeared before him. A small gust of wind shook her dangling earrings and James watched them move, as if hypnotized.

"This cannot be," said Radha sadly. "We are from very different worlds."

"How does that matter?" James heard himself ask

hopelessly.

"We speak different languages, follow different religions, come from different cultures. How will we ever reconcile the two worlds for our children."

"Then we will have no children."

"My roots are in Bangalore. I couldn't leave this city."

"Then I'll uproot myself. Not that I love England less but I love you more. I'll quite literally be *Bangalored* and wouldn't give it another thought."

"You say that now but you will be frustrated. It will make you miserable."

James tugged at a lock of her hair and said, "I cannot think of anyone else I'd rather be miserable with."

"Does this count as a proposal? That I'm your most preferred person to be miserable with? Very well, but we are not having a big, fat Indian wedding. And if you utter the words 'destination wedding', I will reconsider my affections for you."

"I'm only particular about the bride. I care a fig about the wedding. We can just exchange vows at a temple or a church altar, for all I care."

"Oh! I love church weddings. I find the part where the pastor says: 'You may kiss the bride' so romantic."

"One doesn't need a pastor for that. That can be easily arranged."

And, as James bent down, the church bell began to peal.

Surely that was an auspicious start to their wedded life. Why was the ringing getting louder and more insistent though?

James woke with a start. It took him a few minutes to get his bearings. It had been a dream. Too vivid, but only a dream. He laughed shakily as he ran his hand through his hair and then noticed his flashing phone before he heard it again. So it had been his phone and not the church bell. What an unfortunate moment for his phone to ring. Just when his dream had gotten interesting. He hit his palm to his forehead and picked up the phone without looking at who was calling.

"Hello?" he said groggily.

"Hello, James. It's Patricia."

*

James walked around Ulsoor lake the next morning. He wanted to clear his head. He had just called Radha and told her he needed to rush back to England on an emergency. He was touched with the concern in her voice when she asked him if everything was well. He had assured her it was, but that he needed to go back immediately. He hadn't been able to explain why to her. He knew she wanted to know what happened and he could practically see her feelings change from concern to bewilderment to hurt. But there were too many things for him to process and he just couldn't talk to anyone at the moment. Not even Radha.

The lake was serene and the early walkers had not yet arrived. He had been here once with Radha. He wanted to run and she had accompanied him saying she would only walk while he ran. Eventually, he abandoned all plans of running and just walked around the lake with her. It was a beautiful sight, the lake. With its islands over-ridden with trees, the sun glinting off its surface. When they had been there, there had appeared to be a boat race on. Radha had told him that the lake club belonged to the military and it was soldiers on the boating team who were participating in the race. He remembered Radha having called the soldiers' arms sinewy and he remembered teasing her about ogling men. And he remembered how she said she never left behind her phone when she was walking as she wanted the steps to register on her health app. That it wasn't enough that she knew she had walked, but she wanted the recommended ten thousand steps to register on her phone so she could see it! He had loved that about their conversations. They were meandering, going nowhere at all, but always delightful. Something about their conversations had always reminded him of lazy afternoons spent sipping beer.

He navigated through the rush of walkers and joggers. This was where Radha had pointed out a young man who had caught a few fish in the lake and set up a small stall by the pavement. James remembered marveling at the young man's enterprise and also being surprised to learn from Radha that anyone with a skiff could go into lake and fish, no permits required. This was where she had stooped to stroke a few puppies under the chin. Here was where she had bent and re-done her laces. And this was the bench she had sat on and watched the water in silence. Wait, not just sat on. She had apparently, and surprisingly, come armed with a newspaper which she had spread on the bench and then sat on the paper explaining she wasn't sure what dirty behinds might have perched on the bench before her and she wasn't going to risk infecting her clothes. Even now, through all his despair, James smiled at that. She probably belonged in an asylum, did his

Radha.

Except that she wasn't *his*. Transformed into an *other* by his own self. All they had seemed to be at end now. Ended by her stricken, hurt silence that he would never forgive himself for. For as long as he lived.

Should he just have told her what had happened? Would she have been able to understand? Especially after what they had shared the previous night. His stomach twisted with desire even thinking about it. Through the haze of his confusion, he acutely felt his love for Radha. But what was he going to do now? He felt his life had been upended. Like a new swimmer picked up and thrown into the deep end of the pool. Just one momentary lapse, and everything had changed.

CHAPTER *18*

Hello darkness, my old friend.

Simon and Garfunkel

___

The weekend had been absolutely terrible but Radha had survived it despite the Guantanamo Bay-style questioning of her mom and Paati on why she seemed off-colour. James had called and messaged her many times but she had neither picked up nor responded. The messages she had cleared without even reading them. She didn't trust herself. So, she was just not going to have any conversation with him. There would come a time when she would forgive him for walking out on her without any explanation, but not just yet. She wasn't the Buddha. She had gone from euphoria to despair overnight, quite literally, and she felt used.

Radha did manage to drag herself to work on Monday. The coward in her wanted to stay home. But who was it that had said, "No matter what, get up, dress up and show up"? She would do exactly that. There was no way she was going into hiding like a criminal. Besides, she could hardly call in sick. Broken hearts didn't count. And life went on, or so she had been told.

When she got into work, Alex looked at her in concern and asked if she was okay. He must have known James left abruptly. She smiled bravely and he left it at that after patting her hand. That was the great thing about Alex, he had that greatest of quality among friends — the quiet assurance that he was there if Radha needed him but he wouldn't pry. In any other circumstances, Radha would have told him but since this was related to his workplace as well, it was too weird to talk to him about it.

With the issue being too close to Alex and Lakshmi being away on her vacation, Radha felt quite alone. She could have confided in her grandmother but she just didn't feel up to the task. And telling her mom would only have made Revati go ballistic and then Radha would have to stop her mother from jumping on a plane to England to ask James some uncomfortable questions. Revati was always up for a good fight and, where her family was concerned, she was quite the tigress.

Usually Revati bustled through life, running from one place to another, full of life, speaking to someone here, charming someone there, but it was in these moments that her true mom emerged. The woman who was fiercely loyal to her family and would take on the world for them, the woman who believed life was too short to not take sides, the woman nobody should mess with.

*

Radha decided to channel all her energies into work. Perhaps if she immersed herself into her work, the pain would go away. And so, that's what she did for the next couple of days. She remembered her schoolmate, Dheeraj, was visiting from Australia and would be in Bangalore the next day. She would unburden herself to him. Though he was in a different country, Dheeraj and Radha had remained very close friends. He was a no-nonsense person, never tolerated fools gladly, picked up quarrels with no thought to whom he might offend and always defended the causes he believed in. But, above all, he was the kindest, most helpful person Radha knew. A good Samaritan to one and all, he could be held up as an example to be emulated from almost any pulpit. He was a preacher's delight. Helping a friend's mom sell her place since she was alone or giving legal advice to someone who was in trouble, there was no length he would not go to, to assist a friend. Radha was doubly glad he was coming. She was earlier going to introduce James to him since their visits coincided, but now she would just badmouth James to him. Nothing like spewing some venom to feel better. And no better person to do it in the presence of than Dheeraj.

She made plans to meet him over text and continued her work. Never before had a sales proposal held such little promise, but one had to do what one had to do.

*

Radha met Dheeraj in the late evening the following day at Koshy's Restaurant. Koshy's is an old favourite of many Bangaloreans. Having served dignitaries like Nehru, Khrushchev and Queen Elizabeth II, the restaurant is an integral part of old-Bangalore, the Bangalore that stays the same in the middle of rapid change brought about by IT parks and SEZ areas. The signature fish and chips served there is legendary. But more than the food, people keep going back to this restaurant because of the memories they associate with it. Generations of Bangaloreans have dined on the eclectic menu offered here under the tall ceilings from which hang large, creaking fans. It is these die-hard customers that define, by their loyalty and love, the essence of the restaurant.

Radha and Dheeraj had fond memories of this restaurant as well. They had eaten here often when they were teenagers and this was the place they always met whenever he visited Bangalore from Australia where he now worked. They caught up with what was going on with each other. Radha resolved to hold off on the James fiasco till later in the meal. Speaking of it now would just derail the whole conversation and make it depressing from start to finish. She would tell him later.

"You know, Radha, you should get married soon. I could do with some 'balti khana' sometime soon," said Dheeraj using the Hindi words to mean food served out of a bucket. Dheeraj was from the North of India and he and Radha were always teasing each other about where they came from. In this case, Dheeraj was teasing with a reference to South Indian weddings where food was quite often served out of large stainless-steel containers shaped as buckets. He always called South Indian food by that name though he ate it with much relish, being a long time Bangalorean. In turn, Radha usually ribbed him about how aggressive he and his fellow North Indians were. "Always ready to battle without any cause," she would tease him.

"Why should I get married just so you can eat our food?" Radha asked Dheeraj. "You could easily marry a South Indian girl yourself or, easier still, gate crash a Southern wedding. It should be easy if you get caught. Just hit a few people and stick your fist under the noses of others."

"Yeah, yeah! Because we Northies always fight and you Southies are the very epitome of culture, refinement and restraint, right?"

"I didn't say that," said Radha with a smile but the smile didn't reach her eyes.

"Okay, what's on your mind? You aren't yourself, Radha."

And Radha poured her heart out to Dheeraj. She told him everything including recounting most of the silly conversations she'd had with James. And how it had all ended. Right after she had laid her heart at his feet, he had trampled all over it. She felt used and as she admitted as much to Dheeraj, she realized that she had never really acknowledged this to herself.

Dheeraj sat back and looked at her sympathetically. But he was always one to inject levity into dire situations and make them seem less sad. "You discussed Lucifer with him? What were you thinking? How does your dog make for a good conversation? You must have sounded like those annoying moms who bore everyone with stories and photos of their children. No wonder you drove him away. Either that, or you were epic*ly* bad in bed. Forcing him to run for cover right after."

Even Radha had to laugh at this. Though the possibility that he was right sent an arrow of pain through her heart.

Dheeraj continued, "You should have sung some Carnatic music to him or enticed him with Bharatanatyam. Didn't you also, like all good South Indian girls, learn music and dance? You should have struck some seductive poses like a modern-day Indian goddess."

Radha chided, "Firstly, don't be blasphemous. Secondly, you do know that Bharatanatyam largely depicts stories from our epics, right? It's not like belly dancing that one could be enticed by it. If you looked beyond using cuss-words that invoked incestuous relationships with one's mother and sister, you might have known that, you know."

"Nothing gives me more satisfaction than to curse when I am annoyed," said Dheeraj simply. "And I hate it when you do that. Just assume that I curse and fight and am an uncouth ruffian while you are the epitome of culture."

"And now you are mad at me." Radha laughed. "You have been most wrongly named. Imagine naming you 'patience'. What a bitter disappointment you must be to your parents."

"Never mind them, Radha. They've learnt to live with their disappointment. Anyway, it was silly of them to presume me to be of a calm temperament when I was just 11 days old. Now, about this fellow who's broken your heart. I hope you aren't going to mope about him for all eternity. Clearly, the guy is a jerk. You are a huge pain in the wrong place, but you deserve better than this guy. I can re-arrange his face for you, if you want. It might be some consolation."

Radha laughed. "You're sweet. But he's back in England and we aren't going to waste any more time or money on him. I feel better after speaking to you about it. As for James, I wish he goes to the devil."

*

He was going to the devil. The road to hell truly was paved with good intentions, thought James to himself. He had done what he had done only for Radha's sake. But his good intentions had surely broken her heart. He had been home a fortnight now but till now he was immersed in all the work that his new situation had meant. Between that and his office work, he had blocked Radha out of his mind, focusing on the here and now, focusing on what needed to be done. Luckily, Mike had been most understanding of his situation so he had been able to juggle everything on his own. He hadn't involved his mother too much, though he could have used her advice. His mother had never been very fond of Patricia and he didn't have the energy to fight unnecessary battles. The body blow life had given him still had him reeling.

But through all his confusion, the sustained emotion was the loss he felt where Radha was concerned. He missed her. God, how he missed her. And what worried him most was that she didn't know how he felt. She had told him that she loved him, and he hadn't gotten a chance to let her know that he loved her more. After she left that night, he had planned how he was going to declare his own love for her the next day but then Patricia's call had thrown everything out of gear. And now Radha didn't know. She probably felt ill-used by him. She would not answer his texts or messages. He had a feeling she had blocked him. He should have just shown up at her doorstep before he left for the airport that day. He wanted to do it since he had been such an ass when he had called her to let her know he was leaving, but he never had the courage. He didn't want to create a scene in front of her lovely family. He had no idea how they would react. They were from a completely different culture. He didn't know if he'd get Radha into trouble. Perhaps if he had known which room was hers, he might have thrown a stone in through the window, or climbed up using a convenient vine, as heroes seemed to do in novels and movies. But he hadn't. He had been the very opposite of a hero. He had broken her heart and he had, quite literally, flown away. Yes, he had been in a turmoil, but that was no excuse. He could see that now when he had gathered his senses. He could have been a lot more mature about the situation. Not quite so self-absorbed.

But while the tectonic shift in his life had brought about Radha's loss, it had also brought him immense joy and hope. Notwithstanding the fear, uncertainty and a crisis of confidence, the joy was there. He could not change that. He would not change that.

CHAPTER 19

Paropakaaram Idham Shareeram

Ancient Hindu Philosophy

Radha always missed her dad. It was like a dull pain in the background that never went away. It had become a part of her now and, in an odd way, actually kept her connected with him. She could see his face clearly even now; the image had never blurred. And at every crossroad in her life, she would always ask herself how her father would have done things, and she would be guided by the answer.

But today, she thought only of him, and nothing else. She thought of what he would tell her now. How he would interweave stories from his childhood and youth, his experiences and his failures to create almost a playbook of how one's life must be led. What one must do if their heart was broken. There was nothing she would prefer more, right now, than a conversation with him.

Kalyanam was born in a small village in the picturesque Palakkad district in the state of Kerala. Vast expanses of paddy fields surround the village he grew up in. The village itself shares its name with the river Kalpathi, one of the tributaries of the Bharatpuzha river of Kerala. Palakkad is close to the border of the neighbouring state of Tamil Nadu and the language spoken here is actually Tamil, rather than Malayalam which is the language of Kerala. In fact, during the British reign of India, India was governed in provincial borders created by historical events and political and military compulsions of the British Raj and in those circumstances, Palakkad came under the Madras Presidency. After India achieved Independence, the new government realized that state borders needed to be re-arranged, but the basis of reorganizing was only decided by The States Reorganization Act, 1956 where India's states and territories were organized on linguistic lines. It was in this re-organization that Palakkad, though Tamil-speaking, was merged into Kerala and till today, people who hail from there speak an interesting mix of both languages that still provides laughter and comic relief in Indian movies and literature.

It was in this milieu that Kalyanam grew up. He, and his eleven siblings, were born the children of privilege. Their father was an important, extremely affluent and educated landowner. Radha's father had an elephant as a pet when he was growing up and his mother needed the help of an assistant to put on and remove her jewels during the course of the day. But, when half of the children were still very young, their father got entangled in a protracted legal battle. Being bull-headed and not agreeing to any efforts of mediation, Kalyanam's father lost all his money and brought his family to penury. Thus it was, that Radha's father, before he was seven, had seen life take a dramatic U-turn and had gone from having an elephant as a pet to going to bed hungry as there was no food in the house. Radha always thought that these circumstances forged her father's character and made him accepting of the cards dealt to him in life. He took everything in his stride, never whining, never missing a step as he marched on regardless of what was thrown at him.

He had wanted to study to be a doctor but since the family didn't have the money, he gave up that dream without a demur and settled on botany instead. Some of Radha's fondest memories of him were of walking with him while he rattled off the botanical names and common names of all plants and flowers growing along the road. They used to talk all along the route. He would tell her his favourite English songs, how to distinguish an eagle from a common kite, how to recognize and avoid the poisonous Datura plant and not be fooled by its beautiful flowers. Their walk was a microcosm of their lives: Radha learned much from him as she dotingly listened to him, trying to grasp all he was telling her and commit it to her memory.

He had studied at the Victoria College in Palakkad and it seemed like the college's motto 'Labunter et imputatur' which meant that 'life's moments slip away and are laid to your account' found a deep resonance in Kalyanam's philosophy. He had made each moment of his life count. He had always recounted to Radha that, in the absence of parental guidance since his father was too distraught after losing everything and his mother had been too busy keeping the family together, his teacher had been the words of wisdom painted onto the local temple's walls. And so, it was that he had learned 'paropakaram idham shareeram — this body is meant to be used in the service of others — and he had lived that value all through his life. Helping everyone, asking nothing for himself. When he had passed away, Radha and her family were surprised by the outpouring of grief and affection that people felt, all of them recounting the many ways Kalyanam had touched their lives.

Radha would remember him in his white *veshti*, a cloth tied around the lower half of a man's body, and his white holy thread going across from his left shoulder to his right hip, as he chanted his prayers for an hour in the morning. Nothing would make him miss his prayers and if he had to go somewhere early, he would get up that much earlier to ensure his prayer routine was not affected. But the day that began with prayers, almost always ended with a small drink. Radha had asked him about it when she was much younger. How the two worlds seemed too different and Radha remembered him invoking his favourite Hindu god, Shiva, who had always had a preference for *soma*, an intoxicant. In fact, there was a Shiva temple in India where the offering to the Lord was alcohol. Radha had listened to that last bit with a great deal of amazement.

What had always amused Radha about her father was his devotion to *Rajaji*. Chakravarti Rajagopalachari was an Indian politician, independence activist, author and historian. And Radha's father had worshipped him believing him to be a visionary, brilliant beyond imagination and wise beyond the collective wisdom of his politician peers. He could do no wrong in Kalyanam's eyes and many of Kalyanam's statements would start with, "But Rajaji said…"

Kalyanam had been a taciturn man, never expressing an opinion even though he had one. Perhaps it was his prayers and chanting that gave him his calm. He would never engage in a war of words with anyone. He would hold his tongue and keep his unshakeable peace. The only person who received his pearls of wisdom had been Radha herself and she had inculcated most of these habits and traits. Except for her habit of arguing—that she had learnt despite her father. But in everything else, she emulated him. And so, Radha always dressed for dinner. Always tried to conduct herself in a manner that was above reproach as her father had told her she should always be able to look anyone in the eye. She tried to give many her ear but few her tongue, her father's favourite repetition of Polonius' advice to his son Laertes, though this she did less successfully than the rest.

He had truly been a man among men and Radha had never thought she would get over his death. Through that, Revati had helped Radha. A picture of dignity in her quiet grief, Radha's mom had steered Radha through a time when she had felt like curling up and dying. Always more attached to her father, Radha had truly begun to understand the tower of strength her mother was only after Kalyanam's death. And ever since, she and her mom had been very close. There was the ganging up with Paati and teasing Revati, that never went away, but Radha knew she could battle the world with Revati at her side.

And thinking of battling brought James to mind. As her thoughts moved from her parents to James, Radha's pain also changed shapes from the amorphous, dull, bitter-sweet pain of the memories of her father to the clear and sharp pain that came when she thought of James. A pain that made her heart stop, one that made her gasp for breath as if she was suffocating. Had she been an idiot, like all the women she laughed at, and gone and fallen in love with a no-good blighter? Subconsciously, she had always realized that they seemed like soulmates, finishing each other's sentences, liking the same literature, sharing favourite quotes; it had almost seemed they were made for each other. And now, life was looking really bleak. It had been two months since James left and she was still miserable.

She had gotten on with her life, but there were pockets of emptiness that she was just not able to fill. She would be laughing or immersed in something and suddenly, like a bolt from the blue, a wave of sadness would hit her. She had been stubborn and refused to return any of James' calls and still deleted his texts without reading them. There was, at the back of her mind, some guilt associated with her refusing to have anything to do with him but she always suppressed that burst of conscience. What he had done had been unforgivable and she wasn't large-hearted enough to forgive him. That she could hold a grudge for this long was a revelation. But, knowing she was wrong, she perversely did nothing to change herself.

Lakshmi had tried and talked to her to get Radha to unburden herself. But apart from the facts, which by now she had told Dheeraj, Alex and Lakshmi—her closest friends—she wasn't able to explain the pain she was going through. Something told her that her hurt pride had also a small part to play in her state of mind. They'd had an amazing night and then he had walked away. But she couldn't bring herself to admit this flaw in her character to even her closest friends. They walked around her on eggshells, carefully skirting any reference that might upset her. She loved them for their empathy as they avoided all topics that were remotely connected with James. And so, she cried alone.

It was such a secret place, the land of tears. The Little Prince had got this right, and it had taken her heart to break for her to fully comprehend what Saint-Exupery meant.

Radha hadn't noticed the thick cloud cover that had come on suddenly till she heard Revati shout to her to get the clothes in. This was a perennial problem for Bangalore homes. The weather was so unpredictable. It will be sweltering in the afternoon and one hour later there would be a downpour. While the downpour would bring welcome relief from the heat, it almost always had Bangaloreans scrambling to bring the washed laundry in before they were soaked in the rain.

If ever a city needed people to own dryers, it was this.

Radha got up when Revati hollered the second time and rushed to the veranda to bring in the laundry. She heard her phone ringing in the room incessantly. It stopped, then started again. Dumping the clothes onto the couch in the study, she rushed to pick up the phone. It was Lakshmi.

"How many times have I told you, Lakshmi, that you don't need to ring more than once unless it's an emergency? I almost tripped and cracked my skull in getting to the phone because I thought someone was in such a rush to reach me!"

"Don't be so annoyed, Radha. I just thought you hadn't heard with all the thunder and rain lashing down."

"There's no rain here yet. Though it is threatening to come down pretty badly," said Radha, less annoyed now.

"What were you doing?"

"Just sitting around," said Radha, and silently added *moping* to herself.

"I hope you weren't thinking of that blackguard."

"Mm-hmm," said Radha unintelligibly. "Looks like I have call waiting, shall I call you back?"

"Okie-dokie, catch you later."

Radha checked whose call she had missed. Alex. She decided to call him later; she really wasn't in the mood. She sat near her window and looked out. It was quite windy; she should go and check if all the windows were fastened, they might start banging against the frames if this wind got worse. The dried leaves were dancing in the wind, tossed here and there and moving as though in a dance choreographed by nature. A stray piece of paper joined in, determined not to be left out but by virtue of its heavier weight couldn't quite match the litheness of the dry leaves. It had gotten quite overcast and the cool wind blew Radha's hair across her face. This was Bangalore at its beautiful best and, despite herself, Radha's mood improved. She would go make herself a cup of tea. There was no situation in the world that couldn't be improved by a lovely cup of tea. Smiling, Radha unfolded her legs to go downstairs when her phone rang again. Alex again. She had better pick up. He rarely called twice unless it was something that needed to be taken care of immediately.

"Hey, Alex!"

"Hey," and an uncharacteristic silence after that from him.

"What's up? Or did you just call to hear my mellifluous voice?"

"Err, I just needed to add someone to this call. Will you hold on, Radha?"

"Sure."

After a few seconds a voice said, "Radha?"

A voice that seemed to be from a place far away. A voice that still pierced through her heart. A voice she had hoped to forget. A voice that made her sit down as her knees gave way under her. But the only voice that could say her name that way. Radha remained speechless. She had lost track of time.

The voice said again, even softer, even more unsure, "Radha? Are you there?"

She hung up the phone. That traitorous Alex would pay for this. But her even more traitorous heart was pounding. She could hear it in her head. How could he do that to her after all this time? How could he turn her carefully settled world topsy-turvy with just an unsure 'Radha'? She had to get out. It seemed like the walls were closing in on her. All her senses seemed heightened. The wind was now whistling in her ears. She could hear the mewling of a cat somewhere which Lucifer had also picked up and his ears perked up as he let out a low growl.

Radha threw on a jacket and grabbed her car keys. Lucifer followed her. "I'm going for a drive, Amma! Paati!"

Revati and Paati came rushing to the door.

"Look at the weather, Radha! It's going to pour. Why do you need to go out now? It's quite unsafe. And you know our trees in Bangalore. Their branches break off and fall apart in this weather all the time. Go later," said Revati.

"Please, Amma," was all Radha said. But Revati and Paati both knew that determined look in her eyes. She was going to go out, no matter what they said. So Paati just said, "Drive carefully. Keep your phone with you and come back soon."

Radha kissed them both and left. As she got into her car, Lucifer jumped in too. She could feel the tears streaming down her cheeks, Lucifer would never desert her. He put his paws on her lap and licked at her face. She kissed him back and put him firmly back in his seat.

She called Alex. "What the hell were you thinking?"

"Sorry, Radha, but he seemed so desperate and sad and he told me why he had walked away. You should hear him out."

"He can go to hell, for all I care. And I thought you were my friend, Alex!" Radha hung up on him. She backed into the street and then drove away. She had not gone five hundred metres when the downpour began.

Chapter 20

*Every gambler knows
That the secret to survivin'
Is knowin' what to throw away
And knowin' what to keep.*

The Gambler, Kenny Rogers

———————————

She was soaked through and cold as she shivered and sat down on the pavement near the Attara Kacheri, the High Court of the state of Karnataka of which Bangalore was the capital. This was where they had walked hand in hand after their date. This was where James had kissed her. Driving through the rain had not improved her mood. She had loved and she had lost and she could say with certainty that Tennyson was woefully wrong. She could very well have done with not loving James at all.

She had thought things were in control, that she had put the pain in her heart behind her and that she was past caring, till today. When she had heard his voice say her name. *Radha.* And then unmindful of the inclement weather, she had got into her car and been drawn here.

She turned her eyes in the direction Lucifer was looking when he growled. She squinted as the person was still in the dark and behind a sheet of rain. And then Lucifer started wagging his tail.

"You!"

James stepped into the light under the street lamp. Had he grown even more handsome?

She heard him say, "What light through yonder window breaks?"

She laughed bitterly. "I never liked Romeo and Juliet. I told you that but you might have forgotten."

"I haven't forgotten a thing you've said to me, Radha."

"I suppose I should be flattered, but my broken heart tells me that this is just one more of your pickup lines."

James flinched when he heard the bitterness behind her cruel words. But he was responsible for that bitterness. "You know that's not true, Radha. You did appear just now like a light to me; at the end of the darkness your absence has put me in. Whether you like Romeo and Juliet or not, this much is true. And I do remember every small part of our ridiculous conversations. It's what I've missed the most these past days."

"You know, James, it was our mutual love for literature that drew me to you, we got exactly what the other was saying. But you took my heart and crushed it under your Converse shoes when you walked away. Yes, I do remember the shoes you were wearing that last day. So, now your quoting Shakespeare is just pissing me off. Pardon my French."

She continued, "How are you in India, anyway? And how did you know where to find me now?"

"I came to see you," said James softly.

"All the way from England?" asked Radha incredulously but her heart soared.

"Yes," and James offered no further explanations.

"And how did you know that I was here?" asked Radha with her eyes narrowing suspiciously.

"I didn't. You hung up on me when I had Alex call you and I just came here. I have very fond memories of this place. I've thought much about it. It's imprinted on my mind so much that I might actually know it better than most Bangaloreans."

Radha ignored his reference to the time they were here last. It brought too much pain. Instead, she said, "I guess I shouldn't be surprised that you were sneaky enough to reach me through Alex."

"You gave me no choice, Radha. You have not read a single text of mine or returned a single call. I had to do something."

"Why?" asked Radha softly. "Why did you want to see me?"

James saw a single tear roll down her cheek and he felt like a heel. He had done this to her. *Will she ever forgive me?* "Because I wanted to explain myself."

"There's nothing to explain, James. I placed my heart at your feet and you walked all over it. Remarkably, life does go on. And so, here I am. But I really have nothing else to say to you."

"Admit your pride was hurt more than your heart, Radha."

She sucked in her breath. This was the last straw. Who did this chap think he was? She tilted her face up and said with all the dignity she could muster, "Did you have anything else to say to me, James?"

James groaned. He was not handling this well at all. "Radha, I'm sorry. I didn't mean that the way it sounded. It's just that I did do a horrible thing but you never gave me a chance. I called you almost immediately after but you wouldn't pick up. You haven't read my messages. You never pick up my calls."

"Fine! I'll admit it, James. In the spirit of *To thine own self be true*, yes, my pride was hurt too. But that doesn't change the fact that I was hurt too, James. You crushed me. I get that you didn't return my feelings, but there must have been an easier way to let me down. Not just walk away without any explanation. Do put yourself in my shoes. You were the worst sort of cad, James. And it was my pride that allowed me to pick up the pieces and start again. So, don't take that away from me. My pride was all I had."

"I'm sorry, Radha. Sorry seems very insufficient. But there's nothing else I can say. The circumstances were such that I lost my head. You never read my messages so you don't know why I walked away."

"I'm listening now," said Radha as she crossed her arms in front of her chest. The rain had stopped now and she was glad of that. She had put on her most superior air but being drowned in rain drops didn't allow one to look regal. She shivered involuntarily.

"Can we get a coffee someplace first? You are cold and this could take a while."

"I'm not going anywhere with you. If you think you can sweet talk me with your false charm, I'm over that now."

"False charm? Is that an accusation?"

"Is that an admission?" countered Radha.

James smiled sadly at that. "This is one of the things I love about you. You must have the last word no matter what the circumstances are."

"Unfortunately, James, I am in no mood to discuss my many failings with you."

"Yes, I can see that. You look like a thundercloud. But this time I'm not running for cover. It's been so long since we saw each other."

Radha said, "As far as I am concerned if we never saw each other again, it would still be too soon."

James let out a tired sigh. "Please, Radha. Let's get some coffee. You will catch a cold. Do you know any coffee place which allows pets?" he asked looking at Lucifer who was occupied in licking his hand.

Radha glared at her disloyal dog but relented. She was really beginning to shiver now. "Yes, there's Urban Solace. I'll drive us there."

They drove in silence and Lucifer sat on James' lap continuing to lick his palms and to snuggle against his chest. Radha swore to feed him less for a week as punishment. The one living being who she never thought would be against her. Ungrateful, wretched Lucifer.

A little while later, when they were seated and warmed by steaming cups of coffee, James said, "I have a daughter."

Radha spluttered and her coffee almost went flying. "What?"

And then James poured his heart out. He told her everything. That night, after Radha left, he got a call from Patricia, his old-time acquaintance. They had known each other off and on but had not been in touch the last year or so. But the last time they had met, over a year ago, it had been at a bar and both had been a little drunk and one thing had led to another and the evening had finished off in a manner neither had planned. Of course, James had met her the next day and apologized and she had assured him there was no need for an apology and she was absolutely okay with her and James not seeing each other again. No hard feelings. James had left it at that and the next time he had heard from her had been the night she called him when he was in India.

She had been distraught. She had been diagnosed with end-stage cancer. James didn't know what to say and was just starting into blank space when she had told him why she had called him. Apparently, she'd had a baby as a result of the night they had spent together. She never told him because she didn't want him to be obligated in any way to her and the time they had spent together hadn't really counted for much. The baby had been an accident, and she had decided she would care for it.

James had been stunned beyond belief, he told Radha, having found out he was a father. He had just sat there, saying nothing as the room spun around him. By the time he could gather his senses to tear Patricia apart for keeping this from him, she told him why she had reached out to him now. The prognosis for her cancer was very bad and the doctors hadn't held out too much promise. Patricia knew her days were numbered and she wanted to make sure her daughter was looked after and had called James to ask him to adopt her and bring her up.

"You can see, Radha, why I seemed to be in a different world that day when I called you just before leaving for England. I just had too much on my mind and couldn't think straight. Besides, my life was in tatters. I didn't know if I was coming or going. I had no idea what I was going to do. I had no idea how my life would change. So, I just couldn't say anything to you. Even though I could feel your hurt over the phone and it was breaking my heart."

"What did you do?" asked Radha in a small voice.

"I'm bringing her up. I've moved her in with me. Patricia does come and visit but she doesn't keep too well and isn't able to do much. So, for all purposes, I am a single parent. It's been a hell of a ride these last two months but I don't regret it for a bit."

"What's her name?"

"Evangeline."

"That's a beautiful name."

"She's in England now with her nanny, staying at my Mum's place for a few days till I came to meet you. I've had a hell of a time explaining to my folks why I must leave her and come to India."

"And why have you come, James?"

"Because I love you, Radha. And I didn't tell you that before. I did mess up that one day and I know you hate me for it. But I have been trying to reach you desperately these last few months. To explain to you. To tell you how I feel. To tell you that I love you madly, with all my being. What I did was unforgivable, Radha, but you have been very unforgiving."

"Isn't there a contradiction in that, somewhere," said Radha, smiling sadly.

"It doesn't matter. Nothing matters except for how I feel about you."

"How did it get this hard, I wonder. It was always easy with us, that was our thing."

"The course of true love never did run smooth."

"If you quote Shakespeare once more, James, so help me God, I will dump this coffee on your head."

"I think I'd prefer your anger to this cool indifference I am sensing now. So, yes, I'd rather you dumped the coffee on my head than be this distant person you have become."

"What do you want me to say, James? What are you asking of me?"

"I don't really know what I'm asking. I have a daughter; I know it won't be fair of me to expect you to take on that kind of responsibility. Or to be understanding when I have Patricia to worry about too. I can't desert her in her dying days. And anyway, all of this is moot since we are on different continents. So, I really don't know what I'm asking, Radha. I just know that I had to find you and tell you how I feel and to let you know that I'm so very sorry for hurting you even though I did it unintentionally. Above all, I just wanted to tell you I love you. All those things you said to me, I feel them too, only ten times over."

"Thank you for coming all the way to explain to me, James. It means more to me than I can tell you."

"That's all? We have to try and make a go for it. I can't give up on the promise of us. You make me want to be a better person."

"I've seen *As Good As It Gets*, James. Please don't try and pass off that dialogue about wanting to be a better person as your own."

"I wasn't. And this just proves my point, we are soulmates. We complete each other's thoughts and words. We love the same things. Please don't do this, Radha. You'll love Evangeline too."

"I'm sure I will. I bet she's adorable, she's yours." It was as simple as that, Radha realized. If she was James', she would love her.

"And?" James asked hopefully.

"A few months earlier, I would have accepted you, James, warts and all, but there's a chasm between us. I'm also responsible for that chasm, it's not caused by you alone. But it seems like a bridge too far, across that. There were always things that divided us. Our nationality, our culture, our language, our religion, our upbringing but I had begun to feel all that doesn't matter. And it didn't, truly. It doesn't, even now. But if we can't trust each other, the chasm only gets wider and we will end up hating each other."

"But I do trust you," said James as he reached across and held her hands imploringly.

"Not enough to tell me what was on your mind the other day."

"That was a momentary lapse of reason, Radha. How long should I pay for that?"

"Like I said, James, it's not you alone. I didn't trust you either. If I did, I would have given you a chance to explain yourself but I just shut you out. I can't trust myself to do the right thing anymore. My pride got in the way. And you having a daughter is to be considered too, James. You aren't footloose and fancy free anymore, are you? I just don't think we are ready for anything else. We can continue being friends, but I think that will be too painful as well."

James slumped back in his chair. Suddenly, he looked haggard. Radha almost reached out to embrace him but stopped herself. They were on different paths that ran in parallel lines. Their paths could not converge. Mrs Ahmad had taught her that in geometry in school—parallel lines did not meet. No matter what her heart said, her mind told her this. She hadn't been thinking when she thought they could make it work. It would never work. Suddenly the distance between them seemed much longer than a painful flight. It was much more than that. She had to get out of here. She had to leave when her sanity still prevailed.

"I am leaving, James. I trust you will buy me our last coffee. I thank you for coming all the way here to tell me what happened. It really means more to me than I can express. But nothing will come of this. I'm sorry you came so far for nothing, but I'm glad you did. I would hate to part from you in bad blood. That would be an insult to all the time we spent together. I wish you all the luck, James. And Evangeline is one lucky girl to have a father like you."

She bent down and kissed James lightly on his cheek, her right hand softly brushing his other cheek, called to Lucifer who hesitated to leave James' side but came away when he sensed Radha's mood. She stepped out. It had begun to rain again.

*

As James watched her leave, he remained rooted to the spot. He should get up and theatrically run behind her and hold her hand. Not let her go. It always worked in the movies. But he just sat there watching the glass pane from which he had got his last glimpse of her as she had walked out of his life. He watched as a rain drop made its way down the pane, weaving through other water drops, gently but inexorably. Pulled down by gravity, irrespective of its own will. James felt a kinship with the droplet. He knew what it felt to be dragged down like that.

He stepped out. The rain, which had stopped when they were inside, had started to fall again. But more gently. He looked around. There were broken branches and mini carpets of leaves around him. People, who had gone inside to avoid the worst of the rain, had begun to stir, stepping outside to check for damages to their store awnings, or if anything had fallen on their cars. A group of strays cavorted in the middle of the traffic-free road, playfully nipping at each other. Bangalore had a washed, clean air. Somewhere along the road he had travelled, James had come to love this city. He hummed to himself as his feet dragged him to the nearby Ulsoor Lake.

Anything but love,

Anything but hearts that beat like thunder,

Anything but love would be enough,

For anyone but you.

James stood near the lake and watched the rain beat gently on the surface of the lake water.

EPILOGUE

ONE YEAR LATER

And a new day will dawn
For those who stand long
And the forests will echo with laughter

Led Zeppelin

Radha sighed as she stood in line at Café Coffee Day. That client meeting could have gone better. And she had spent over ninety minutes on the road to get here. This retail chain serving coffee across major cities of India, almost the Starbucks of India, has been an integral part of the lives of India's millennials. A hangout for many college students, it has seen the forging of strong bonds of friendship over idle hours spent sipping coffee, especially in Bangalore where the chain had started. The philosophy of the chain has never been to hurry customers out, so cash-strapped students would share just a single cup of coffee and gratefully spend hours together in the welcoming ambience of the shop. Radha knew some of her entrepreneur seniors, who, having little money for office space, would meet and brainstorm here. Many a business idea had been conceived here, many dreams had been shattered here, many hopes had been kindled here. Many a heart had been stolen here as couples exchanged sweet nothings over a drink. And, of course, many a heart had also been broken here.

If only the founder of the chain would have thought to check with millennials and GenX of India what his store meant to them, he would have known the eternal gratitude owed to him. Perhaps then, he would not have done what he had. Perhaps the love, admiration and gratitude people felt for him would have held him back.

She found an empty table. She was not looking forward to the drive back. Madan had called in sick and she had taken a cab. She was now going to have to take another one back, if she found one at this rush hour. She was halfway through her food and had just taken a rather uncomfortably big bite when she heard a soft, questioning voice.

"Radha?"

She stilled. Surely, she was hallucinating. She turned, cheeks puffed with food, praying, *let it not be him, let it not be him!* But of course, it was. James Rutherford in flesh and blood. Looking more dashing than she remembered. She gave a weak wave but couldn't say anything as her mouth was full. Of course, this would happen. The man would magically appear like Apollo, all lean and muscled, and her stupid heart would still beat wildly, *and* she would be caught at her worst—mouth stuffed, unable to speak. After what seemed like a mortifying ten minutes, but was actually less than thirty seconds, she smiled and said, "Well, hello," and then, "How the hell are you here?"

"It's very nice to see you as well," said James with his characteristic smile. Shouldn't Radha have forgotten his smile by now? *Idiot girl! Be a sucker for punishment. Moon over him.*

"Sorry, I'm just taken aback. When did you get to India?"

"I've been here just a little under a month."

The unspoken question in Radha's mind was, "Were you planning to call me?" but she just continued staring at him and then realized she was being rude. "Do sit! That is if you have nothing else to do. Are you with someone?" she stammered. She really was an idiot.

James drew back the chair opposite Radha with easy grace and sat down. "I had told Alex, but I guess he thought it unwise to tell you."

Dear Alex. He had seen a tormented version of Radha he had never seen before for the better part of the last year. Of course, he would not tell her.

"It must have slipped his mind." Well done, Radha, let him know that he isn't that important and that we aren't always discussing him. "How long are you here?"

"Err, actually, I've been given a three-year assignment to head up our India operations. So, I'm here for a while."

"Wow! Congratulations! That seems huge. Well done."

"Thank you! I guess of the two roads that diverged into the woods, I've taken the one less travelled," he shrugged.

"With due respect to Frost, this is hardly the road less travelled. We have plenty of expats in Bangalore." And she thought to herself, you folks are expats but if we work in your country, we are immigrants. Then she mentally scolded herself for being uncharitable. It was hardly James' fault that the terminology was discriminatory.

"Yes, I guess that's true. Incidentally, I'm in your campus

itself at Embassy Golf Links."

"Oh! We didn't run into each other for so long."

"It's a big campus."

"True."

And after that sparkling exchange of conversation, both fell silent.

Finally, between uncomfortable silences and unremarkable bits of dialogue, James gleaned that Radha was headed back to the office and offered to drop her. Radha was surprised to find out James was driving himself.

"I love driving," he explained, reading her thoughts. "And we drive the same side, so it's not tough."

"But Bangalore traffic must have taken some getting used to!"

"At first. But I'm quite at home now."

They reached the car and James opened the passenger door for Radha and closed it after her. As he walked around to his side, she watched him from under her lashes. When he turned on the ignition, Radha was stunned into silence by the music that was playing. A R Rahman's *Rehna tu*.

"I remembered some of the lyrics, googled and found the song," James explained softly. "I love the song, play it on loop often." But what he left unsaid was that it reminded him of Radha. Not just that she had told him about the song before he had kissed her, but also that the song's lyrics could have been written for her; they were that close to what he felt for her.

Radha asked him, "How's Evangeline?'

"Wonderful. She's loving it here." The adoration in his voice sent a pang through her heart.

They passed the rest of the journey in relative silence. Radha looked out of her window the other way. It was unfathomable why she was tearing up but she would not let him see. The traffic had cleared up remarkably and they made it back in much lesser time than Radha would have imagined. James drove up to her building's parking and looked straight into her eyes.

"It was lovely seeing you, Radha. I cannot tell you how much. I was gathering up the courage to call you and each time I thought I would, I chickened out. I must thank providence that we ran into each other. You look as wonderful as I remember you to be."

Radha just stared at him, saying nothing.

"Cat got your tongue?" James asked sadly.

Radha only said, "Thanks for the ride," and started alighting.

He was by her side in a trice, holding the door open. "Will you come home tomorrow, Radha? I would love for you to meet Evangeline. I'll make dinner."

We are not the same persons this year as last; nor are those we love. It is a happy chance if we, changing, continue to love a changed person.

Somerset Maugham

Author's Note

The only important thing in a book is the meaning that it has for you.

Somerset Maugham

I wrote this book as an ode to Bangalore, my most beloved city, and as an ode to the world of IT, which has been my partner in crime for the majority of my working life and has taught me much and taken me to many places. And as an ode to our shrinking world. May we all come together as one, blurring boundaries and striving to the ideal of 'Vasudhaiva Kutumbakam'.

I hope that some part of this book resonates with each of you and holds meaning for you. Be it in the city you love. Or in a profession that was responsible for you meeting someone special. Or the magic of friendship. Or the steadfastness of family. Or the thrill of flirting with a good-looking, intelligent person. Or the first flush of love. Or the devastation of heartbreak.

If I made you think of any of these things with a smile, I will consider my work begun.

ACKNOWLEDGEMENTS

I thank my family—your every quirk breathed life into my characters. Thank you for the madness. Especially my daughters who, when I asked them how they liked the book, nonchalantly answered, "We've read worse". I thank my husband who, when I expressed a desire to be famous, promised he would print a large obituary for me in all dailies across the country when I kicked the bucket. Clearly, love is a many splendoured thing.

I thank my dogs; you teach me what it is to live with unjudging love, unflinching loyalty and without malice. It will be my lifelong quest to become a little like you.

I thank Bejoy George, Saikat Dey and Shyam Monappa; you will never know what a big role you played in me completing this book. And all the early readers of my book: Shanti Menon, Reshma Hegde, Subramaniam Ambale, Sridhar Gopalakrishnan, P Ramani, Rengarajan Iyengar. I thank Padma Ganapati, my earliest editor and the entire Leadstart team.

I thank all the authors who transport me to different worlds and inspire me every day: Jane Austen, Daphne du Maurier, Georgette Heyer, PG Wodehouse, Thomas Hardy, Somerset Maugham. The last in that list once remarked that 'The ability to quote is a serviceable substitute for wit'. I have used that serviceable substitute lavishly in my book and I thank you for that. From the bottom of my heart.

I thank Julia Quinn; you do not know me, but you are the Dronacharya to my Ekalavya.